No Country for Old Men

No Country for Old Men

Ernie Savage

Cover photograph(s) by the author and Nick Savage.

Troubador Publishing Ltd
Unit E2 Airfield Business Park,
Harrison Road, Market Harborough,
Leicestershire LE16 7UL
Tel: 0116 279 2299
Email: books@troubador.co.uk
Web: www.troubador.co.uk

ISBN 978 1 80514 365 9

British Library Cataloguing in Publication Data.
A catalogue record for this book is available from the British Library.

Printed and bound in Great Britain by 4edge Limited
Typeset in 11pt Aldine401 BT by Troubador Publishing Ltd, Leicester, UK

To all the church people of Cleadonbridge.

Sailing to Byzantium

William Butler Yeats

That is no country for old men. The young
In one another's arms, birds in the trees,
—Those dying generations—at their song,
The salmon-falls, the mackerel-crowded seas,
Fish, flesh, or fowl, commend all summer long
Whatever is begotten, born, and dies.
Caught in that sensual music all neglect
Monuments of unageing intellect.

An aged man is but a paltry thing,
A tattered coat upon a stick, unless
Soul clap its hands and sing, and louder sing
For every tatter in its mortal dress,
Nor is there singing school but studying
Monuments of its own magnificence;
And therefore I have sailed the seas and come
To the holy city of Byzantium.

O sages standing in God's holy fire
As in the gold mosaic of a wall,
Come from the holy fire, perne in a gyre,
And be the singing-masters of my soul.
Consume my heart away; sick with desire
And fastened to a dying animal
It knows not what it is; and gather me
Into the artifice of eternity.

Once out of nature I shall never take
My bodily form from any natural thing,
But such a form as Grecian goldsmiths make
Of hammered gold and gold enamelling
To keep a drowsy Emperor awake;
Or set upon a golden bough to sing
To lords and ladies of Byzantium
Of what is past, or passing, or to come

Chapter One

Sunday 8ᵗʰ July 1962

'It's sad really, my last time.' Greg Thomas slid into the back pew in St. Columba's church next to Steven Darlington, just as the procession entered for Evensong and Benediction.

'So, you're off to London tomorrow?' his friend asked.

'Yep. Well, Wednesday. Graduation day before yesterday and then hey ho for the big wicked city. I want a clean break. Cleadonbridge is not big, or,' he winked at Steven, 'wicked enough for me. You're stuck with it for another year of course, doing the Cert. Ed. course.'

Steven whispered to Greg, 'I can't see Anna.'

'No? Well she may be a bit upset, but I did say I was going to make a complete break.'

'You've chucked her?' Steven was amazed.

'Yep.'

Steven was silent, contemplating the now familiar scene. The procession was the usual one of five men, wearing white, lace fringed cottas over their black cassocks. Two of them might almost have been serving at St. Columba's since it was built in 1885; he could never with certainty remember their names. There were also younger

1

men; the acolytes came first, carrying candles in tall brass holders, then the other servers. Behind them, wearing a splendid, fading green cope, came the Vicar, though Father Mainwaring was always styled "parish priest". The cope might really date back to the church's opening.

He remembered how he had found it a complete contrast to his church in Devon. Mr. Butler, the vicar of his home church, was small and rather fussy; Father Mainwaring was tall and rather ascetic. Mr. Butler almost gabbled the words of the liturgy and Steven was reminded about a story he had read when studying A level History, that Henry VIII had promoted a particular priest because he was able to get through the Mass in a shorter time than any other, allowing the King to get out hunting sooner. Father Mainwaring spoke slowly and reverently; the familiar words seemed to have a greater meaning. Some of the service was intoned, which seemed at first rather curious. Sometimes, Steven was never quite sure why, Father Mainwaring and the curate, Father Beddoes, wore the curious headgear called a biretta. When his parents came to stay, his mother had been a little disturbed by all the "romish" ceremonial; his father had been quite baffled and claimed that the incense had given him a headache. They were glad that he was still a practising Anglican, but would have preferred him to have attended somewhere like the church in their home village in Devon. On other visits they had avoided churchgoing. Three elderly men sitting in the choir stalls sang the office, but as the young boys who sang treble at the High Mass could not or would not attend in the evening, half a dozen women sang soprano. They were not allowed to sit in the chancel so were hidden in the Lady Chapel.

Three years earlier, queuing to register for geography at the University of Cleadonbridge, he had got into conversation with Greg, a fellow fresher, who was to study economics. Greg had commented that the Gothic excrescences in the Victorian building were rather like his church. Steven had assumed that he came from some distant place. It was over three hundred miles from his home to this northern city and he was surprised that Greg's church was, as he put it, "just round the corner".

'Are you a churchman?' Greg had had asked.

'Yes, most Sundays at our local parish church. Mum teaches in the Sunday School; Dad is a Churchwarden.'

'What services do you have?'

'What do you mean?'

'Is it Morning and Evening Prayer with Communion tagged on sometimes?'

'Well, yes. And there is the early service of Holy Communion.' Steven had assumed that all Anglican churches followed this pattern.

Greg chuckled. 'We have three Masses on Sunday mornings, Low Mass at 8 o' clock, Parish Mass at 10.00 and a High Mass with all the works at 11.00. At least we can only have the full High Mass if we can get a third chap to do subdeacon; we've only got Father Mainwaring and Father Beddoes. In the evening we have Evensong and Benediction.'

'So, it's Roman Catholic then?'

'No, not RC, but AC.'

'AC?'

'Anglo Catholic. Smells and bells, holy smoke and water, ritualistic, whatever you want to call it.'

'Oh.' The idea had appealed, perhaps it been some sort

of adolescent rebellion. Not that his mother was especially opposed to high church practices, although some of the congregation fulminated about a nearby parish where the rector had introduced "Sung Eucharist" as the principal Sunday service, but it might shock someone like Mrs. Watson if he were to speak of going to "Mass". Or perhaps it was the force of Greg's personality that propelled him to St. Columba's.

'Why don't you come along on Sunday? Where are you living?'

'Boulton Hall.'

'That's only a hop, skip and a jump from here and close to my home. I live with my parents and it's, well two or three hops and skips to our church, St. Columba's. Tell you what. After we've finished here I guess we are both homeward bound. We can walk there. We can have coffee at our place and then stroll along to Columba's.'

The University is on the edge of Belford Park, three miles from the city centre. It had begun as a university college in the 1930s and was housed in a converted Victorian industrial school, built in the same style as many civic institutions of the period. Hospitals, prisons, schools and colleges all were of the same grim Gothic formality. More modern buildings had been added, some in the neo-Georgian style, which was favoured at the time of its foundation. Some of the villas on the edge of the Park had been acquired; one housed the Geography Department.

After the registration formalities were completed, Greg led the way through the rather bewildering collection of buildings that made up the University and out onto Park Crescent.

'Here we are! Thomas Towers.' They were standing in front of a three storey Victorian semi detached stuccoed villa, with a small formal garden.

'Thomas Towers?'

'That's not its real name. It's simply 23, Park Crescent. But it is a bit of a towering pile, don't you think? Anyway, come in!' Greg ushered him down the large and gloomy hallway. In some ways it was not unlike his own home, *Green Haugh*, although that was built in the 1930s and was a detached house in a small country town.

'We spend most of the time in the back here.' He opened a door into a large room furnished with a mixture of antiques and more modern furniture. On one wall was a large chest.

'That's an eighteenth century Lancashire mule chest,' commented Steven.

'Mule?'

'The top drawers are dummies aren't they? It's really just a deep storage space,

Greg smiled 'You're right. I'd show you but I'd have to take all these things off.' He gestured at the rather motley collection of ceramic ware and family photographs.

'That's just like ours. My mother came from Lancashire originally.'

'I haven't the slightest idea where this came from. I assume it was handed down from some long-dead ancestor.' He turned to Steven. 'I'm a bit fed up of dwelling here in the past, surrounded by generations of Thomases and others. I did put in an application to LSE, but the APs were agin it.'

'APs?'

'Aged parents. They think it's a bastion of Communism and they are of course Conservative. I might have stuck out, but it would mean leaving Anna and…' His voice tailed away. For a moment he seemed rather less self assured.

Steven had nothing to say. In many ways he could wish he was in a similar position to Greg, but Exeter wouldn't have him. He turned away and looked out through a bay window overlooking a surprisingly large garden. It was autumn, so the flowers were past their full glory, but Steven could see that it must have been a riot of colour. Again there were similarities; the garden at *Green Haugh* was a particular joy for his parents.

'What a wonderful display of dahlias', he commented. 'And the Michaelmas daisies, they're just past it now, but they must have been magnificent and…'

'They are rather good. Mother does it all. What was it Shakespeare said? Some are born gardeners, some acquire gardens, and some have gardens thrust upon them.'

'*Twelfth Night* of course, but it was about greatness.' Steven smiled.

'I know that,' Greg's comment was almost a sneer. 'But the idea can be transferred. Mama is a born gardener. Papa has had gardening thrust upon him. But I am not prepared to acquire a garden or have the blessed business of gardening thrust up on me. I leave it all to them.' He peered out of the window. 'It doesn't look as though they are at home next door. So I cannot yet introduce you to Anna, my little sister.'

'Does she live in a separate house?'

'She's not my actual sister, but we grew up and played

together as children. It became a sort of joke that we were brother and sister. We are both only children you see.'

Steven, who was also an only child, was silent. It might have been good to have an honorary sibling, but he'd been perfectly happy playing with the boys and girls in the village and had recently started going out with some of the girls.

Greg laughed. 'I ought to stop calling her "my sister", as we are going out together.' He laughed. 'It might be seen as incest!'

'You mean that you and her…' Steven left the sentence unfinished.

'No, we don't have sex, yet at least; she's only sixteen. We are though, as they say, going steady. But I promised you coffee. Make yourself at home here while I get it going.'

The coffee, when it arrived, was real coffee in a tall ceramic pot with matching cups. 'You'll drink it black.' Greg's remark was a statement, not a question. In later years Steven came to prefer black coffee, but he had always had it with milk, and he found this difficult to drink, but somehow he could not argue with his new friend. Greg pushed a plate towards Steven. 'Here, have a chocky biccy!' The biscuit ameliorated the bitterness of the strong black coffee.

Once coffee and biscuits were finished, Greg rose. 'Come on then, we'll meander towards town and see St. Columba's.'

Steven had arrived the previous day and had, at his mother's insistence, taken a taxi from the railway station out to the University. 'You can't take all that clobber from the railway station three miles out on a bus. Here!' She pressed a couple of pound notes into his hand. He was excited and somewhat anxious, so had hardly noticed the streets of the city, which he was visiting for the first time. Cleadonbridge had not been his first choice; that would have been either Exeter or even Bristol and he had applied to both those universities. But he had been refused, so made a late decision to go to a further corner of England. His A level grades were better than the school had predicted; he had achieved 80% in geography, and Cleadonbridge was happy to offer a place without an interview. Many years later he discovered that they had had an unusually low number of applicants with the required grades.

On his arrival he had chatted to some of the other students who were in Boulton Hall and had seen them and others at breakfast, but had made no plans other than the required attendance at registration, so he was quite happy to follow Greg's suggestions. They now walked into the city, leaving the wooded gardens of Belford Park, and reached Belford Avenue, which he learned later to refer to as "the Boulevard", a broad tree-lined street leading from the city to the Park. Occupying a commanding position at the park gates was a church with a tall broach spire, the nave and chancel built of yellow sandstone with red sandstone dressings and a tiled roof. Steven guessed it was late nineteenth century.

'Is that your church then?' asked Steven.

'No, that's St Peter's. It's very low.' Greg rather dramatically deepened his voice as he said the last word. 'This area was once really posh – look at those houses!' He pointed along the road to the elegant Victorian terraces, most had three storeys, although the semi basement gave them an additional level. 'Servants in the basements and the attics; masters and mistresses on the other floors.'

Steven saw that paint was peeling, some widows were cracked and other panes of glass had been replaced by pieces of wood. The door of one the houses stood open, revealing a gloomy hallway. Children playing some sort of game rushed out screaming with laughter. Steven saw many of them were black. Behind these houses were streets of smaller, terraced houses. A strange odour compounded of damp, dust and rot hung over the area. There were other rather more nauseating smells, which he did not like to consider. It must really be rather insanitary; he supposed it might be described as a slum. Steven began to think he didn't much like Cleadonbridge; it might have been better to hang on and see if a place had become available in Exeter or, perhaps he might have waited until next year. With his having good marks at A level, he might have been accepted at Bristol.

Greg broke into his thoughts. 'Before the war our family lived here, number twelve, there.' They had reached the city end of the Boulevard and the houses here were late Georgian rather than Victorian.

'I guess they were wealthy then?'

'My grandfather was in shipping, but they moved out about the time my parents got married in 1938. Even then the area was going downhill and after the war there were all these immigrants from the West Indies and...' He left the sentence incomplete, and Steven felt no inclination to ask Greg to complete it. He was uncomfortable with his own feelings on immigrants. The previous year had seen the Notting Hill race riots.

Stanley Street, which cuts across the line of Belford Avenue, now came into view. The line of the Boulevard continued towards the city centre as Gilbert Street, and Steven could see more Georgian terraces and the classical portico of a church of the period.

'Is that your church then?' He pointed.

'No, it's St. George's. This is ours!' St Columba's was not a very impressive building and, although they were now opposite the church, Steven had not noticed it.

'Oh, bloody hell!' Greg swore.

'What's the matter?'

'Those kids!' He strode across the road. Steven followed hesitantly.

Three or four primary school age children were rushing in and out of the church. As they disappeared inside, the noise of their hooting echoed round.

'Just stop it. This is a house of prayer, but you are making it…'

Steven assumed he was going to add "a den of thieves" but the children interrupted him.

'Y're only going on at us because of the colour of our skin.'

'That's got nothing to do with it. You are disturbing other people. Go!' His tone was almost threatening and they fled, one of them turning to make a "V" sign before disappearing down a side street.

Once inside and his eyes adjusted to the gloom, Steven saw that there were several old ladies at prayer, so Greg's harsh admonishment of the kids was perhaps appropriate. One of the ladies was in fact Afro-Caribbean. None went into his own church in Devon for private prayer, although it was open during the day, but the only visitors were tourists and others interested in its long history. Of course, they might offer a prayer, but it would not be their primary purpose.

So had begun Steven's association with this church. He gazed round now and remembered his amazement at the riot of colour and imagery. The exterior of common brick, with dressings in red brick and stone, had not prepared him for the glorious richly coloured interior with its Victorian polychromy and wall paintings. The roof timbers and the panelling between them were all also painted. In the nave were the Stations of the Cross and on the west wall the Feeding of the Five Thousand. The gilt reredos with tiers of saints was especially striking. On his return home he had found his parish church St. Mary Magdalene's dull, not only in its staid ritual but in its furnishings. Of course, in medieval times there would have been a riot of colour. A tiny fragment of one of the wall paintings had been discovered. So fragmentary was it, that no one knew what it displayed; some claimed it was part of a Last Judgement.

On his first Sunday he attended High Mass and met Greg's parents. Mrs. Thomas was a lady who was perhaps not fat but was the sort that his mother described as "well upholstered". She was dressed in a rather old-fashioned flowing dress and had a commanding presence. After Mass, as many stood chatting at the back of church, she announced, 'I'm going to stop coming to this church, Father.'

'Oh dear! Why is that?' asked the priest.

'I'm always being asked to buy something. It's marmalade today but other times it's been, well, all sorts of things.' She turned to Steven, 'Are you the lad Gregory was telling me about?

'Yes. I came along with him today.'

Father Mainwaring turned to Steven and shook his hand. 'Hello. Nice to have you with us. May I ask you your name?'

'Steven Darlington.'

Mrs Towers asked. 'Have you met my husband? He's Vicar's Warden.'

The Churchwarden was standing back smiling, but he extended his hand. 'Welcome to St. Columba's Steven.'

'My father is Vicar's Warden in our home parish.'

'Jolly good! We'll have you in that role one day.'

'What, here? I am only at the university here; my home is in Devon.'

'Perhaps you could help out with the serving here. You've seen that we have quite a team.'

'Yes, there do seem a lot. We have nothing like that at home. At,' he hesitated before he used the word, 'at Mass there's only the Vicar.'

'Do they call the service "Mass" or "Holy Communion"?'

'Holy Communion. I suppose we're pretty Low Church.'

'I was too until I met the lady who is now my wife.' He gestured in her direction. 'She seduced me. My parents were a bit upset because this place was thought to be almost Roman. Do you like it here?'

Steven was not quite sure how to answer this. 'Greg mentioned that I might join the servers, but he seems to have disappeared. It's all a bit confusing and…'

'Alfred Carter organises them. Excuse me a moment, Steven.' Mr. Thomas called, 'Alfred!'

A tall man of about thirty, still clad in cassock and a short surplice, turned. 'Yes, Mr. Thomas?'

'I want you to take Steven here and get him into the servers' team.'

'OK. Steven, or is it Steve?'

'Steven, please.'

'Come along.' He led the way to the parish hall.

Greg, who had disappeared after the end of the service, leaving him rather at a loss, was there with some men about the same age. 'Hey!' Greg called. 'So you've made it; I told you to come along with me after Mass. Still, you've got here now.'

Steven recalled no such comment from Greg.

'Anyway, now that you're finally here, meet Jim Dewhurst, Ted Harris and Forbes Jackson. This is Steven; he is reading geography at the University and I think he might like to join the team.'

'Hello!' The all shook hands. Jim was rather fat and jolly; Ted was thin and seemed almost to be sneering much of the time.

Forbes spoke first. 'If you are to serve the altar you must learn how to do it properly.' He spoke forcefully and in an almost peevish manner. 'And you must study this.' He held up a slim, dark book.

'Give it a rest, Forbes,' Greg almost shouted. 'Let's just do the basics.'

And so Steven was patiently instructed on the various duties of serving at Mass.

It was not on that first occasion that he met Anna, but the following week when she arrived at High Mass with her formidable mother. Mrs. Ashworth was dressed in tweeds and commanded the situation with an almost imperious look. Greg introduced him to them, describing Anna as his "little honorary sister" and her mother as "My dearest second Mama". Anna's father was not present. He only comes to church for hatchings, matchings and despatchings, Anna told him.

Steven thought Anna attractive; she was wearing a smooth fitting red and white striped dress with a billowing skirt, which she showed to advantage by a little pirouette. Her blonde hair was rather longer than was fashionable. She turned her head and brushed her hair back with her hand as she gave him a sidelong glance over lowered lids. She somehow managed to look innocent and seductive at the same time.

'So, you're Steven.' Her smile was almost suggestive.

She was Greg's girlfriend. Steven hurriedly looked at him. His expression was in part amusement, but there was an implicit threat. Greg could, he imagined, turn nasty if crossed.

It was typical of Greg that he should dragoon Steven into joining St Columba's. Steven and whoever was his girlfriend at the time were often invited to join Greg and Anna, except that the conversation was often something such as, "We're going to see *The Merchant of Venice* at *The Kirkgate*. I assume you and Ros will come?" *The Kirkgate* was the repertory theatre and both Greg and Anna were very interested in the theatre; both had been involved with their schools' dramatic societies and the theatre workshops at *The Kirkgate*. Greg joined the University Dramatic Society on the first day and became a leading light in it. Steven instead became involved in the University Rambling

Group. Anna, who did not go to university, was active in the Youth Theatre.

Steven forced himself back to the present and realised that Evensong had finished and Father Mainwaring and the server, Denny, had taken the Blessed Sacrament from the aumbry and placed it on the altar.

'He's not up to it!' Greg muttered. Although he often served at Mass, Steven seldom assisted at the evening service, only attending when there was a meeting afterwards, as there was that evening, but Greg did and had been training Denny for the role of MC.

'Who, Father Mainwaring or Denny?'

'Denny.'

'What's he doing wrong?' Steven asked.

'I've told him a dozen times that he mustn't… Oh, what's the use?' Greg thrust his head into his hands, though whether this was a gesture of despair or assuming a prayerful mode was impossible to tell.

'Well, you can't be serving the altar here if you are going to London. It'll have to be Denny and the others…' And me, Steven thought. He'd occasionally been corrected by Greg when he had not done things exactly like the book, though Forbes was fussier.

The choir were singing *O salutaris,* the first lines made him think.

Oh saving victim, opening wide
'The gate of heaven to man below.'

Was this church his gate to heaven? The last lines struck him even more.

Oh grant us life that shall not end
'In our true native land with Thee.'

Was his true native land here in Cleadonbridge? Or in Devon? Of course, the words referred to heaven, but yet… He forced himself back to the present, and to Cleadonbridge and to concentrate on the service, the words that had over the three years become so familiar. The Divine Praises were being repeated; it all seemed interminable, but they were now ending.

Blessèd be God in the Virgin Mary, Mother of our Lord and God.
Blessèd be God in the angels and in the saints.
Blessèd be God.'

Blessèd be God indeed, he thought. Afterwards, he could not remember whether he had sung the last hymn, *Soul of my Saviour, sanctify my breast.* His mind was in a whirl. Greg was going away; he had detached himself from Anna and she was now…

The billowing clouds of incense from the service drifted upwards and dispersed, revealing the painted roof timbers; some of the congregation were now moving out of St. Columba's church by the side door, which led into the garden separating the church from the Vicarage where the monthly meeting of the *Pusey Society* was to take place.

Jim Dewhurst and Ted Harris approached. 'We've decided to give it a miss this month. We're going into town.'

'What are we going to have this evening? I do hope it's not more of that dreadful modern music that young Thomas played.' Mrs. Hallworth, a middle aged lady of decided views, had not enjoyed the records of *Das Lied von der Erde* that Greg had brought along to the discussion the previous month.

'Mahler is not really modern. He was about the Edwardian time, I think,' her friend, Mrs. Walmsley, suggested as they filed across the garden towards the Vicarage. Like Mrs. Hallworth, she spoke with the refined accent imparted by Cheltenham Ladies' College. Her clothes were not exactly shabby, but were definitely of yesteryear and, as Steven had noticed on previous occasions, there was a slight odour of mothballs.

A tall and rather stately Afro-Caribbean lady, Fiona Edwards, joined in. 'I could not make any sense of it. I like a jolly tune.'

'It would be nice to have Elgar; he was Edwardian,' put in Mrs. Hallworth.

'Perhaps, but I think this evening Father Mainwaring is going to speak on how Christianity was brought to England,' Mrs. Walmsley said.

Greg had caught up with them. 'Oh, Saint Augustine and all that jazz. Sixth century I think?' He turned to his friend.

'No, you're wrong there, Greg.' Steven spoke rather sententiously. 'There was a Christian presence in the later period of Roman rule in Britain. And much of the north was christianised from Ireland.'

'Ya mean when the Paddies came over after the famine?' They had been joined by Denny, Fiona's son, who was about sixteen and had just left the parish school. He had removed his cassock and cotta that he had worn when serving at Benediction.

'No,' put in Steven patiently, 'that was in the nineteenth century. We are talking about the Dark Ages.'

'When everyone was black like me?' Denny guffawed.

Mrs. Walmsley drew in her breath audibly. Steven was never quite sure what people like her thought about the fact that many in the parish were from the West Indies. No outward signs of racism were apparent, but there was a slight distancing from Fiona. In fact, there was normally a physical distance; families such as the Walmsleys and the Hallworths had moved out of the area, as indeed had the Ashworths and the Thomases. But there was also a socio-economic distance. The newcomers were poor and people such as the Hallworths and the Walmsleys were, or had been rich.

'You just mind your Ps and Qs, or I'll give you want for!' Fiona's Jamaican accent came out much more strongly as she reprimanded him.

At this moment they reached the steps of the Vicarage and filed in. Denny and the two students stood aside to allow the ladies to enter. At this moment Anna appeared, running up the path from the road. She was less elegantly clad than normal, wearing trousers rather than a skirt and her hair was not as carefully set as it usually was.

'Oh, there you are, Anna.' It was her mother, who had emerged from the church just in time to see her daughter's arrival. 'I know you are excited, but I do think you might have tried to get to Benediction this evening.'

'Well, Mummy, at least I'm here for the *Pusey Society*.'

'Why are you excited, my dear?' asked Mrs. Edwards.

'I've got an acting job, for the summer season at Southsea.'

Steven turned to her. 'Oh, how marvellous!' He opened his arms and kissed her; the kiss was returned passionately. Greg grinned in a rather enigmatic manner. 'I've been wanting to do that for three years,' Steven murmured into her ear.

'Why didn't you then?' she replied quietly as she drew back from his embrace.

There was a shocked silence, broken by the arrival of Father Mainwaring. 'Do go in, ladies and gentlemen. Mrs. Ashworth,' he turned to Anna's mother. 'I'm sure you and the other ladies will organise the coffee and tea; I'll get the sherry out!'

Steven did not have the opportunity to speak to Anna for the rest of the evening; neither of them contributed to the discussion that followed the Vicar's talk and he avoided eye contact as he made a hurried excuse to leave. Had he really wanted to do that for three years? She was certainly attractive, but it still seemed disloyal to Greg, who might really want to resume the relationship. He put her from his mind, and it was many years before they met.

Chapter Two

Thursday 5th July 2012

'Well, ladies and gentlemen! Here we all are, within sight of the Woodfold Mellor Hall.' Frank Moss is in good form, thought Steven. 'Fifty years ago, almost to the very hour, we all trooped across the stage to shake the VC's hand and become graduates. It seems that we've managed to get as many as possible here on this auspicious day. Sadly, not all of us could get here, some for the saddest reasons.'

Obviously a few of our lot must have died, Steven thought, recalling now that Frank had written that Gerry, Mark and Kate had died; he was ashamed to remember that he couldn't recall the causes of their deaths. Was it cancer like Mary? Frank paused in his speech, carefully glancing at his notes. Obviously he'd prepared this carefully. Steven was not able to recognise everyone. He had been very unsure of whether to come to the reunion, especially after the events of the previous year, so he had arrived at the last minute for the lunch and there had been no time to meet and chat. We've all aged, he realised; could the others recognise him? He had checked in late last evening at the modest hotel that Frank had arranged, and deliberately avoided any contact with the others who were there for the reunion party, pleading exhaustion from the journey. Many of the others had only arrived this morning and this was the first part of the formal programme, not in the rather grandly named *Belleville*, as the hotel was called, but in a new and rather trendy restaurant on the edge of the city's business district. At the time of their graduation, the University had no hall large enough for the Degree Day ceremonies and they had used the concert hall of the local symphony orchestra, which was in the city centre, opposite the building where they were lunching, although this had not been built then. They had what was grandly termed *The Executive Dining Suite*, a private room on the first floor, overlooking St. John's Square. Across the square, now free of traffic, in part given over to an informal market, and on the other side from the concert hall, was St. John's Cathedral with its tall spire. Half closing his eyes, he could imagine it was a medieval townscape, though he knew that the church building was Victorian and was only raised to cathedral status in 1926. But he brought himself back to the present and to Frank's speech.

'We haven't all achieved the great things that we expected…'

Of course, that had been his thing. Unlike Steven, but like most of his university contemporaries, Frank's parents were not graduates and somehow Frank had assumed that they would become captains of industry, or top politicians or something. Very few of them had, Steven smiled wryly to himself; one needed an Oxbridge degree, or the right sort of connections, for that. He himself had always had low expectations, envisaging getting a job in an ivy clad grammar school and remaining there until he retired. It hadn't been quite like that, but he certainly hadn't reached the top. Of course Frank had tried; he fought several elections as a Liberal candidate, never more than slightly denting the majority of the Labour or Conservative party. He had achieved some notoriety at Liberal assemblies, once taking a midnight dip in the nude to... was it a protest or just attention grabbing? He himself had been content with his lot as a lecturer in a small college of further education, not in a big city like Cleadonbridge.

Thoughts of place brought back the words of that poem by Yeats, *Sailing to Byzantium*. It all began sixteen months ago with a series of chance events in which the poem was somehow central to it all. The first verse had been the trigger.

> *That is no country for old men. The young*
> *In one another's arms, birds in the trees.*

We're all old men and women now. He smiled to himself, recalling the last line of that verse, which he had jokingly thought of as the university.

> *Monuments of unageing intellect.*

...monuments. Steven brought himself back to the present. What was Frank saying about monuments? 'Seeing all the monuments of past civilisations we silver-haired chappies...'

Steven saw Dorothy Smith, or whatever her married name was, bristle. She still had the full head of dark red hair she had when a student, or should one describe it as "auburn". Did that come out of bottle or was it as nature intended? The latter seemed unlikely given her age.

'...are not only surfers of the World Wide Web, but of the world itself. I'm hoping to get to Australia this year; it's the only one of the seven continents I've not yet set foot in...'

Well I've beaten you there, thought Steven. But the only reason to go had been the need to visit the boys... His thoughts trailed away.

He may be an old man, but he had a country and he belonged, in a very real sense, to that part of it called Devon. He had felt that his roots penetrated the red soil of the county, but where did he really belong now? But it was a search for a place that had brought him to Cleadonbridge last year; he had hoped for a new start.

He observed that Frank's baggy sweater and corduroy trousers were almost the same as those he would have worn for lunch in the Students' Union cafeteria in their student days. The edict had gone forth that lunch should be informal, but that for the dinner it would be black tie. The latter had caused Steven some anxiety as he did not own a dress suit, but he managed to borrow one from a fellow parishioner who played in an amateur orchestra and was required to wear one at concerts. Steven himself liked to dress well; at least he hoped it was well. He was wearing a lightweight jacket and a tie of a modern pattern and colour; many of the other men were wearing jeans, he observed, and the women's dresses similarly ranged in formality. Dorothy had a very smart summer dress and... But what was Frank saying now?

'Well, that's just about it folks. It's time for din-dins

and I can assure you that it will be better than the food we had to queue up for in the Union Caff. I can see that the minions are bringing the hors d'ouevres.'

Isn't that typical and didn't it exactly explain his reluctance to go to reunions. What was that play by Michael Frayn, where a group of old friends get together? Frayn had said, he recalled, that all they had in common was the "things they had shared earlier whilst at university." *Donkey's Years*, that was it. He'd seen it in Bristol and they'd considered doing it in the village drama group. "Minions"; whoever said that nowadays? Even the word "hors d'ouevres" was rather passé. As was that word. He laughed having hoisted himself with his own petard, as it were. Face it, man, you're an old fogey!

'What's funny, Steven?' The speaker was Dorothy Smith, who was sitting opposite.

'I was just thinking that some of us haven't changed much.'

'Physically, do you mean, or in our views?' Anthony Davies joined in the conversation.

'Both, I suppose. I mean we've all grown greyer but most are still recognisable, although who's the guy at the other end?' He pointed down the table.

'Where? Oh, that's Bob Roberts; RKR Holdings – he's on the *Sunday Times* rich list. That's how I found him and passed his name onto Frank.'

Steven realised his thoughts about none of them having become captains of industry or top politicians was wrong. Bob was a top business man, Frank had tried in the field of politics, and Mike Wilson was a professor. He was the one who had not pushed himself; he had been content with his limited success in a sleepy backwater.

'Bob's changed, like we all have. Wine, women, and song.' Anthony grinned. 'Though you don't look any different; perhaps you have been as pure as the driven snow. We could have been a bit wilder when we were here, but I suppose we were all too naïve to really go for it. Still, I've made up for it since!'

He had been more or less pure and had had a healthy life style. At least, he had been pure until last year… It was difficult to describe to the younger people of today, and he had never tried to explain to his sons Nigel and Paul, that in his student days many of them were inexperienced sexually and remained so until the end of their course. Was it the more rigid ideas of sexual morality or the fear of an unwanted pregnancy? The pill was in its infancy, but condoms, never called that, but "jonnies" or the usual brand name, were widely available in the barbers; sometimes the barber would proffer them with a sly grin, "something for the weekend, sir?" In some ways they envied Jack, a rather wild character in their year, whilst not being sure if what he told them about his sexual conquests was true. He was thrown off the course at the end of second year, but it was because of his failure in exams rather than any sexual misdemeanours. They wanted sex, or thought that they wanted it, but were too… too what? Hidebound by convention? Constrained by religious beliefs or by the girls they might have bedded? Some did certainly. What was the name of the couple in the year above them who had married in the long vacation? By Christmas, Janet – that was her name – was obviously pregnant and her husband, Martin, was very solicitous for her welfare. We were shocked in one part and envious in another part, but certainly didn't want to be in that position. Not that, at least as far as they knew, Jack ever was, but Steven knew that even in those days, abortion was possible, if you knew the right people. He dragged himself back to the present. Frank, whom he was sure had never transgressed that line, was still in full flow, although only to those next to him.

'But old Frank doesn't seem to have changed...' Steven's voice trailed away.

Anthony laughed. 'You mean he was always a pompous ass and...'

'...still is!' They both laughed.

Dorothy broke in. 'I think you are being most unfair to Frank. He's worked jolly hard to get us all together.'

'I suppose so. It's just that...' His voice trailed away. Dorothy waited and looked expectantly. He laughed. 'I suppose I'm just being a grumpy old man!' But it wasn't that. It was all about his feeling a sort of jealousy for Frank and his apparent certainties. Even now, Steven thought, he wasn't sure what he was doing with his own life; or where he was going.

'Did you ever come back to Cleadonbridge, Steven?'

'No, in fact this is very nearly the first time in the last fifty years.'

'I've come back for these reunions that Frank has been organising over the years. You haven't!' She spoke almost accusingly.

'No, well, it's a long way from the West Country. People think that you are there when you get to Bristol, but we are a long way beyond that.'

'I've also to come to meetings in Cleadonbridge in connection with work.'

'What was your work?' he enquired politely.

'I was involved in teacher education latterly and there was a group concerned with special needs which met in various centres all over England.'

'Did you ever go to Exeter?'

'Once or twice, yes.'

'You should have let me know. We might have met.'

'I didn't have your address. But you said that it is very nearly the first time in the last fifty years. Did you have a meeting here too?'

'Yes, a meeting…What about you, Anthony?' Steven asked.

'Oh, I was in town planning and latterly was with the inspectorate, so I gadded hither and yon. I was often able to meet Dorothy. We had some interesting times didn't we, Dot?' He grinned at her.

'Yes,' interposed Dorothy rather tartly, 'as you said before, you've made up for your naivety since! And don't call me "Dot" or I'll dot you one.'

'Hey!' cried Anthony. 'You were just as guilty of naughtiness as me!'

Steven was baffled. It seemed as though they had had an affair. His speculations were interrupted by Dorothy's renewed cross questioning; she seemed to want to turn the conversation away from whatever it was that she and Anthony had been up to.

'So, what was your meeting in Cleadonbridge then, Steven?'

'I thought I'd return and see how the city had changed.' He turned to Anthony. 'See if the town planners had left anything of the old place.'

'Not fair!' Anthony almost shouted. 'Teacher, leave them planners alone.'

'In fact the damage seems to have been minimal, as I saw a year ago. Sorry, Anthony.' It was in fact just over a year ago. A conversation with his sons had determined him; he had posted his letter, made the other necessary arrangements, and set off.

Steven returned to his quiescent state and munched his way through the plate of *Salade Niçoise*, with his mind on the events of fifteen months ago. He half listened to the conversations around him.

'No, it was in second year when we went for that field course in Scotland and old Robbo...'

'He always said...'

'But it was Whatisname, Henry... that got pissed with the lads when we went down to the pub.'

What had he hoped for? Was it to see if there was life in the old dog yet? Was that a quotation from something, or was it Trad or Anon, those great English authors? Had he wanted there to be life... he had hardly articulated, even silently, the word sex. He hadn't had anything even resembling a sexual liaison from well before Mary's death. But last year... it didn't seem quite right and yet... Things were so different now; sex outside marriage seemed to be the norm and many people didn't bother with marriage vows, even when in a permanent relationship. None of his friends ever asked about his sex life.

They had moved on to the main course of *Coq au Vin*, served with new potatoes and *légumes de saison*. He decided to take an interest in the food, which was really rather good. Frank was a good organiser.

'A penny for them, Steven?' Dorothy Smith rather startled him, and he blushed, almost as though she had known what he had been thinking about.

'Tat, tut! Obviously impure thoughts.'

He rallied and even managed to chuckle. 'Chance would be a fine thing!' But he wondered if he did want another chance. He remembered that first evening, chatting about things at St. Columba's half a century earlier, which had somehow, led to... was it a final fling? Although there had been another evening... He couldn't feel ashamed of it but didn't want to repeat it... with anyone. What was Dorothy Smith saying? He had to drag himself back to the present and the excellent *Tarte de Fraises*. He wondered what was in the dish; typically French, it seemed, although he was inclined to think that strawberries were best eaten just as they were. He prodded the dish, trying to get an idea of its content and wondering whether, in spite of his normal preferences, he might try to make it. He hoped Susan Jamieson was picking the last of the strawberries at *Green Haugh*.

'Wake up!'

'Sorry, what did you say, Dorothy?'

'I asked you,' she spoke as to a particularly backward pupil, 'if you don't like this strawberry whatsit? I love it, but you seem just to be playing with it.'

He smiled. 'I was wondering whether I might be able to make it at home; we have, I mean I have, a lot of soft fruit in the garden.'

Their conversation, and the others buzzing in the room was curtailed by Frank's banging on the table.

'Of course, this is the moment when we might give the

29

loyal toast, but that will be more appropriate at dinner this evening. Anyway, God bless Her Majesty! It would also be the time for me to then say, "Gentlemen, you may smoke," but the smoking ban… who'd have thought it? Anyway, that makes it impossible. Any of you who are still smokers will have to curb your desires a little while longer.'

That is a major change, Steven thought. By now most of them would have been puffing away and by the time coffee was served, the smoke would have made seeing across the room difficult. Frank, he recalled, had smoked a pipe, a rather pleasant aromatic brand, sometimes in a large and ornate pipe, very appropriate for the man. Poseur was the word that sprung unkindly to his mind. But what was he saying now?

'Ladies and gentlemen! I thought that as we were all getting on now and didn't want to be gadding hither and yon too much, we'd have our overnight stay in the city centre, and I hope you were all satisfied with the hotel.' There were murmurs of assent, Steven included. 'But we cannot let the occasion pass without paying a visit to our old haunts.'

He wondered what was coming. Was Frank going to suggest they went to some of the dives in the city centre that the "fast" set had patronised? Help! That slang was not even of the period when they were at university; it belonged to the 1930s!

'So, I've ordered a mini coach to take us out to our alma mater. When you have finished your coffee, I'd like you all to follow me. I should point out that the costs of this have been borne by our old friend Bob Roberts who isn't short of a bob or two, if I may be permitted a pun!' There were groans.

He was quite glad to get away from Dorothy; her questioning had been rather intense. On the coach he found himself sitting next to Eddie Saunders. He had always rather enjoyed his company and they chatted pleasantly. Steven knew that he had been a teacher; and had taken the post graduate education course at Cleadonbridge with one or two others in the year. They had kept in touch for a while but had somehow lost contact.

'So where were you teaching?' Steven asked politely. 'I know you started at Henry Danvers School.'

'I was at Henry Danvers for the duration. It was a grammar school when I started and it's now one of the top comprehensives in the country. I went there and sort of got stuck; it was a very pleasant rut to be in. When I was about thirty the head of department retired and I got the job. I lived in Cleadonbridge, in Oakdale. And I was going out with Helen, a local girl. I couldn't be playing the field like you guys who came from further away.' He laughed. 'Helen and I are just coming up to our fiftieth wedding anniversary; I think the girls are planning something, our daughters and their own daughters, our lovely grand daughters.

'Of course I also went into teaching but made a last minute decision to do the education course at Bristol'

Eddie nodded. 'It was mentioned at registration.' He affected a disapproving tone. '"Mr. Darlington has decided not to take the course in the Department," and we did meet several times afterwards.'

Steven laughed. 'Of course. I taught for a while in Bristol, which was where I met Mary, then we moved back to Devon, and I got a job in the further education college near my home village. We've two boys; Nigel is in Australia and Paul is in New Zealand. He's married and he and his wife have twin boys. But Mary died two years ago. You're luckier; Helen is still alive and your girls and their kids all in the area.'

'Hell, I'm sorry, Steven! I didn't want to upset you.'

'It's no matter; I've got used to it all now…'

'Why didn't you write and let everyone know?'

'Everyone?'

'Well, we were a close-knit year group, the geographers of '59. We could have supported you. Of course, you did drift away, even from your friends.' Eddie seemed sorrowful.

'I made a complete break with Cleadonbridge, went back to my roots. This wasn't the place for me.' Steven pondered his own words. He had not articulated that fifty years ago, so it was what he had realised after the events of last year. He had, he supposed, fled from the place, or perhaps the people there.

There was an uncomfortable silence for a minute or two and the chatter from the others surged into the void. The coach made its way through the traffic on Gilbert Street. Steven was very conscious that they were passing the flat… there were conflicting emotions. Annoyingly, they halted just outside it. He hung his head down to avoid the possibility of being seen, even though rationally he knew that he would be unlikely to be spotted.

His downcast manner was misinterpreted by Eddie, who, desperately trying to change to the subject, said, rather too brightly, 'Didn't you persuade me to come to your church somewhere round here? Was it that one?' He pointed to the church they were passing. 'It was very high as I recall.'

'No, that's St. George's. That is, or at least was, very low.' Steven laughed. 'There's St. Columba's, just ahead now, that was where I took you. Very different from your parish in Oakdale; Christ Church isn't it? Do you go there now?'

'I'm afraid not; I don't really buy into that now. Religion seems to bring so much misery into the world. I'm sorry, Steven. Ah there's your St Columba's. You're still involved with the church then?'

'Oh yes!' He drifted off, for there was the familiar façade of St Columba's and again it was recent events there that caused a pang. There had been something, and he had hoped... but what was Eddie saying?

'So are you still high church?'

'Well, I suppose so, not that our parish is really Anglo-Catholic, though it has moved a bit in that direction. But the old distinctions are now so blurred and there isn't that sort of antipathy between the different branches of Anglicanism.'

They were now stuck in traffic at the junction with Stanley Street. St. Columba's was just the other side of the junction, at the city end of the Boulevard.

Eddie chuckled. 'Our Vicar was horrified that I'd gone there.' He nodded towards the church. 'Talked about "Romish practices", and implied I was bound for hell. If hell existed I'd certainly be bound there now as I never darken the door of any church.'

'His sort would never have countenanced the thing that happened in the Cathedral a few years back now.'

'What was that?'

'The statue of Our Lady of Walsingham was taken there. The Dean said it was a tradition of churchmanship that enriches the Church of England. They carried the image in and the people in the congregation were all sprinkled with holy water.'

'I know this obviously means something to you Steven, but it's not really the concern of most people today, if it ever was.'

Steven realised that something like this had been said last year. As they drew away from St. Columba's he remarked sadly, 'It's not quite as high as it was; there are so few in the congregation now.'

'How do you know? Have you been there recently?'

'How do I know what? Oh, the attendance at St. Columba's. Yes…' How far away it seems now, although it had only been just over a year ago. 'I had a meeting in Cleadonbridge and went there on the Sunday. There were still one or two in the congregation from the old days.'

'So you are still very much into religion then, Steven?'

'Why do you say that?'

'Coming to a conference or whatever can be an excuse to get a bit of nookie, rather than going to church.'

Steven smiled ruefully for he had a bit of "nookie" on that visit last year. He was struck, as he had been the previous year, how Stanley Street was a real boundary, not just in architectural terms between Georgian and Victorian, but between gentrified areas such as Gilbert Street and the working class area beyond; St Columba's was in the working class area. He tried to guess how many might live in the parish.

Eddie continued chattering but Steven was miles away; the coach had moved on and they were now nearly at Belford Park and the University. There was St. Peter's and, like last year, there was a banner, this one urging the world to repent. It was here, recalled Steven, that he had begun his silly idea. A walk in the Park and back had sown the seeds of a belief that this city was the place for him and… and that he could somehow reverse the church's decline.

What was Eddie saying? Something about religion again. Repent? He contemplated sharing the meaning of the word as it had been explained by a Canon Theologian in a recent sermon in the village church. It was something about changing direction, but he couldn't remember, and it was probably pointless to discuss it, now at least. Was Eddie trying to convert him? What was it he had said a moment or two ago? "You're still very much into religion…?" His going to church so much that week – he counted… four times… might have been described as that, or was he seeking something?

Steven turned to Eddie with an attempt to widen the argument. 'Does religion have no good in it? A lot of churches now are working to alleviate poverty. Some of the ones in the city are establishing food banks. And St Columba's from its beginnings ran an orphanage and a home for the destitute. I believe that they organised provision of food for the very poorest and…'

'I know, I know, but… Let's talk about something else. Do you remember where this little restaurant is that we are to take over this evening? You've got to hand it to Frank, he does organise these reunions well.'

'I'm not quite sure where it is; near the city centre I think. I did look it up when Frank sent out the details of the reunion. "Greek but with a full range of Mediterranean dishes", they claim.'

'It has an odd name. *Amalthia,* isn't it?'

'That's right.' At least it wasn't that other Mediterranean place where they'd dined last year, Steven thought. He couldn't even remember its name. It might have been better just to have had a quiet dinner that one evening, chatted about the old days in St Columba's, made their farewells so that he could get on with his studies in the library and take his trip to the Lakes.

What was Frank shouting now? He brought himself back to the present.

'Here we are at the gates of Belford Park; we thought that some of you would like to walk the last bit, stretch the old legs, those of still able to walk, that is!'

'You were a keen walker weren't you Steven? Weren't you in the rambling club at university?'

'Oh yes, great rambles over the Pennines.'

'Do you still get out on the hills? I must say it never really appeals to me. It so often rains and blows.'

'I like to go when I can.'

'But it will be Dartmoor and so on now; you won't be visiting the Pennines like you did when you were a student?'

'I was there, on the Pennines… not so long ago, in fact, then later on in the Lakes.'

A holiday?'

'I suppose so.'

'So, are you going to do the walk now then?' Eddie asked him.

Steven laughed. 'A stroll across the park is hardly a walk as I understand it, but it will be good to get out.'

It was a warm sunny day and most got out to walk. They passed the end of Park Crescent. It was along there that both the Thomas and Ashworth families had lived. Of course their parents would be dead by now and as for Greg and Anna… he smiled ruefully. He thought back not only fifty years ago but to more recent events. Somehow in the mêlée he became separated from Eddie and found himself next to Mike Wilson.

'Hello Mike, I believe that you should now be addressed as "professor"?'

'Well, emeritus now.' He spoke somewhat self-deprecatingly, but Steven knew that he was regarded very highly within his field.

'Congratulations anyway,' Steven said.

'Thank you.'

'I've read some of your books. Especially the one about my own part of the world.'

'Which one was that? Oh, of course, *The Significance of West Country Ports in Early Modern England*. Was historical geography your thing then? I can't remember.'

'Not really, I did my dissertation on denudation chronology, but I always found historical geography interesting, and as a teacher you have to be a bit of a jack of all trades.'

Mike laughed. 'You never did any further research then?'

Steven shook his head. 'No time really, and no real drive to do it. I need someone to prod me into action. Anyway, denudation chronology is old hat now.'

But he had taken the opportunity of that visit to Cleadonbridge to explore his academic interests. He had nursed the faint hope that he might even undertake some research.

Mike Wilson was saying something about Steven's former tutor. 'Was that with Ted Robinson?'

'Yes, it was his speciality, and he was damned recently in an article. I looked that up. All his theories exploded!'

'Well, that's what academics do, something that we have to try to get through to first year students, who want everything cut and dried. I blame their teachers.' He grinned at Steven.

'We do try,' he protested.

'But students aren't what they were… but then they never were. Who said that about what?'

'Sounds like something Noël Coward wrote.' Steven laughed.

'You're keen on the theatre then?'

'I suppose I am. I didn't join the dramatic society here, but I've since become quite active in our village group.'

Steven saw Bob approaching. 'Hey there Stevie! I heard you had lost your wife; I'm so sorry.'

He hated this form of his name, but he forced himself to smile. After all Bob was only trying to be kind. 'I'm OK thanks Bob.'

'Well perhaps you may meet someone. Someone to keep you nice and warm in bed!'

Steven smiled ruefully. 'I don't think that's likely somehow.' He couldn't cope with his suggestions about finding a… what? "Girlfriend" was hardly an appropriate term at his age. Was he ashamed of what had happened last year? Perhaps he wasn't ashamed of it; he just wondered if it had been worthwhile, but he had hoped… and on that flimsy basis he imagined new life for himself. Was that why he had made the initial contact? Had he just wanted sex? Or had he hoped for more from the start? If he had wanted to build a relationship with Anna, the opportunity had presented itself that day fifty years ago just before he left Cleadonbridge. He had no regular girlfriend at the time and Greg had just chucked her. But he still could recall Greg's look after the "stolen kiss" in the Vicarage. Steven had spent the three years at university giving way to him, perhaps almost fearing his anger.

The main university building had now come into view. Frank called them to order. 'Well folks, there it is. Our Alma Mater. I thought you'd like a photo opportunity. That Kodak moment, though I guess most of you are digital now.'

Many indeed did take their cameras out.

Eddie had now caught them up and chipped in. 'A nice ramble; just long enough for me and in pleasant sunshine, with the possibility of escape to a bus. None of that traipsing across the moors in driving sleet and gales. I think you told me that you even did that on honeymoon?'

'Fancy you remembering that!'

'Well, you did invite us to the wedding, and we saw you off at the station on a train bound for the north; we gave you a real send off.'

Steven smiled ruefully. 'You certainly did; we told you we were going to Blackpool, but you guessed we were going to the Lakes.'

Steven and Mary had invited a few friends from their respective universities. He hadn't intended to but Mary, who was at Liverpool, had kept up with the ones she knew in the hall of residence there and persuaded Steven to contact the ones he had kept in touch with, although in the event it was only Anthony Davies who brought his girlfriend and Eddie and Helen Saunders that he contacted. Eddie and Helen had married almost directly after leaving university and had invited most of the year to the ceremony. Steven had booked a holiday for the same time so didn't go, but had felt a sort of obligation to invite them to his own wedding and somehow Anthony had been included. He had not considered inviting anyone from St. Columba's. He had some contact with Greg though not with Anna.

'You said you've been to the Lakes, recently.'

'Oh yes, only last year; a sort of spur of the moment decision...' His voice trailed off. He became aware of Eddie's looking at him in a concerned way.

'Yes, I went to the place where Mary and I spent our honeymoon.'

Eddie laid his hand on Steven's shoulder. 'I'm so sorry; it must have been terrible for you losing Mary.'

He said nothing; if Eddie wanted to think he travelled to the Lakes to wallow in self-pity, let it be so. His trip was, of course, for very different reasons, although they came to nothing. Or were they different? Had he been trying to recreate what he had lost? He became aware again of Eddie's hand now on his own in a friendly clasp.

'I don't know how I could cope if Helen died.'

'Don't worry about me, and, if you recall, perhaps from your childhood Sunday School lessons, "Take therefore no thought for the morrow: for the morrow shall take thought for the things of itself. Sufficient unto the day is the evil thereof." I think that, even for an atheist, it's perhaps a good philosophy of life.'

'You may well be right there. It's good that you can be so positive. So did you climb any mountains?'

Steven described the day on Place Fell. 'I was tired, but it was exhilarating. I stayed in town the following day.'

'Where, in Cleadonbridge?'

'Yes, in a little B&B.'

By now they were actually in the university campus and further conversation was lost as they all were pointing out the buildings they had once known so well. No, he didn't wallow in the past that day and his euphoric mood had continued the day after he returned to Cleadonbridge.

'Steven, are you with us at all?' They had reached the geography department and were waiting for Christina Lucas, one of the professors, who was to show them around. Dorothy Smith rather startled him. 'Wake up!'

'Sorry, what did you say?'

'I was asking you that, as you were in teaching...'

'Yes. I'm retired now though.'

'So was it a meeting about education that brought you back?'

'No, it was personal.' He spoke shortly, hoping to stop her probing questions. He laughed; perhaps it has been an educative experience. What had he learned? A bit more about sex? And a lot more about himself certainly, his hopes and even his fears, but more particularly he had learned where he belonged, perhaps where he had always belonged.

'You were in teaching?' He nodded. 'Did you send any of your students here?'

'Some. One of my best ones did his first degree here a few years ago; he's now a professor in Melcester, John Llewellyn.'

The tour of the Department, led by Professor Lucas and the amble around the much changed campus occupied most of the afternoon. Park Crescent, where Anna and Greg had lived had become part of the University. The Victorian villa that had housed the geography department was demolished shortly after their graduation, when the huge expansion in higher education had begun. Now the department was in a ten storey block, which it seemed to fill. Of course in the sixties there were only about thirty in each year and so it was all very intimate; everyone knew everyone else. But the biggest surprise was the laboratories; even their existence was a revelation to him.

Christina Lucas had explained. 'We can conduct a wide range of investigations, such as analysis of water, soil and sediment.' She continued in great detail, but Steven only listened half heartedly. It was all so different from the rather simple methods used by everyone fifty years ago. There was no way in which he could work in these state-of-the-art laboratories, even if he were granted permission. She was darting round pointing out various things. 'Mixer mills for soil preparation, shaking tables vacuum filtration units.'

He recalled his conversation with those two students, what were they called… Josh and Luke. Their specialisms on the human side of the subject had seemed remote from his own knowledge, but he had expected to understand the physical geography.

The mini coach sped back to the hotel, unhampered by rush hour traffic. As he was now on the other side of the coach, he didn't feel it necessary to duck down as they passed along Gilbert Street.

Chapter Three

Wednesday 16th March 2011

'Well Paul, I suppose you might call me a silver surfer.' Steven was speaking to his younger son who now lived in Auckland. He was never sure what his business was. If someone asked Steven he said, "Something to do with computers." Paul had married Sandra, "a Kiwi girl" as he had said to his father. Steven and Mary had assumed that they would live in Britain, but Paul had fallen in love not only with Sandra, but with New Zealand and they had settled there. His business evidently flourished as they had an almost extravagant lifestyle, which Steven had shared for a couple of weeks the previous year.

'Are you enjoying it Dad?'

'Err, yes, I suppose I am, but I'm not telling everyone. I had a letter through the post from Frank Moss last week; he's arranging yet another of those reunions.'

'What for?' This was from Nigel. The boys had set up Skype, so a three-way conversation was possible. It was morning for Steven but evening for both Paul in New Zealand and Nigel, who was in Melbourne. Steven felt he had a much greater understanding of Nigel's work as he was with the Australian Bureau of Meteorology, and he had taught some basic meteorology as part of the geography syllabus.

'It's fifty years, or it will be next year, since we trooped across the platform in Cleadonbridge to shake hands with the Vice Chancellor.'

'We had the Chancellor herself,' said Nigel, 'when I graduated.'

'I remember. I may be old, but I'm not losing my marbles yet and she's quite a glamorous lady. Why did they choose her as Chancellor?'

'I don't know.'

'Are you suggesting that our aged parent is losing his marbles?' put in Paul.

'Sorry Dad, I didn't mean I thought you were old. Seventy is nothing these days. But why aren't you telling anyone?'

'That I'm on the Internet? Because I'd be pestered even more by Frank and his cronies and others. I was cross when he found my name from the Society's list; you know I'm secretary of the local branch?'

'Yeah!'

'And my name is listed, so that anyone wants to keep in contact can find me. I insisted that my personal e-mail was not shown. They have to go to the central website.'

'You'll come up if they Google you too, I guess.'

'I google, thou googlest, he googles…'

'It just means use the search engine of that name.' This was from Nigel.

'I know that,' said Steven. 'In fact, I do it all the time.'

'But why don't you want to go to reunions?' put in Nigel. 'I used to enjoy them when I was still able to get back to uni; they can be quite good for networking. It isn't as if there was any reason to stay there in *Green Haugh* all the time.'

'You're right, since your Mum died there's no reason to stay here and… I'm not exactly brooding but, it's a long way and…' His voice tailed off; he was not sure in his own mind as to why he did not want to return to Cleadonbridge. 'My mother said we shouldn't look back; she never did, and your brother has followed her precepts, even if you haven't.'

'I wish I'd met Granny Darlington,' said Paul. 'She always sounds more interesting than Mum's mum was.'

'She dandled you on her knee, but Nigel, don't you have some memories of her?'

'Only rather dim memories now.'

'But,' put in Paul, 'I do remember how you used to read Beatrix Potter stories to me like she read them to him?'

'Do you remember how we had to make a pilgrimage to Newlands to look for Mrs. Tiggy-Winkle.' They all laughed at the recollection.

'We had some good holidays in the Lakes,' put in Paul. 'You took us up Skiddaw, our first mountain.'

'And we went abroad,' added Nigel. 'What was the name of the holiday village in the Ardennes?'

'Where we ate a lot of coarse pâté and drank a lot of rather rough red wine.' Steven chuckled. 'It was all the local shop provided, and neither your mother nor I wanted to cook. Happy Days!' He sighed.

'Dad?' Nigel spoke gently.

'Yes?' Steven guessed what was coming next. Even though it was now a year since Mary died, Nigel and Paul worried about their father.

'You are alright? It's just that with me being here in Auckland and Nigel in Melbourne…'

'I came on my grand Antipodean tour didn't I, to see you and all the tourist places and to show you that I'm not brooding. I miss your mother, of course I do, but life goes on.'

'So why won't you go to the reunion?'

'I might,' he said cautiously. 'After all it is fifty years… guess what I found on the internet today? I know you aren't churchgoers now…'

'I'm not against it I just haven't time Dad!' Paul spoke defensively.

'You know my views on religion,' added his brother.

'OK, OK. I'm not going to try to try to convert you, but I found the website of St. Columba's that I used to go to in Cleadonbridge and it boasts its main Sunday Eucharist as "Family Friendly, Coffee and Incense". Evidently St. Columba's is maintaining the High Church tradition which attracted me, a sort of rebellion against my mother. But the website was under construction, so it says little more, and the diocesan website gives little help.'

Nigel laughed. 'Well why not go and check it out?'

'Well, I looked up trains, express coaches and driving times – it really is amazing what you can do on the internet. For example, I looked up the times and fares and discovered that if I go via Manchester and book a separate railway ticket it's about half the price of booking a through ticket from here. I don't want to drive; it's over five hundred kilometres.' Steven was determined to use the metric system which he believed should be adopted by Britain to bring it in line with the rest of the world and had adopted his schoolmasterly tone. 'The coach is fine but it's so tedious. Do you know there are websites for travel and accommodation and...'

'Dad, I spend all my working life on computers I know that sort of thing.' There was a slight weariness in Paul's tone.

'I suppose so.' Steven was slightly subdued but rallied again. 'And I found a little B&B in the city; they're quite cheap too, of course the north of England is cheaper, always was... In fact, I've already booked a trip there for this month. I'll have a wander round the old place on my own, though I expect that it will have changed a great deal.'

'Go for it Dad!'

Nigel added, 'Have a great time – send us a post card!'

'I'll do just that. And now I'd better be going. Love to Sandra and the twins. And all the best to you too Nigel, though you have a bit longer before bedtimes?'

'They're safely tucked up in bed! And Sandy and I'll be on our way there too. Night!'

'But I need to check something over before tomorrow, Dad. Great to chat. Night!'

Steven knew his sons were worried that he might be sitting brooding. His sigh when they had been talking about holidays was heartfelt, but they had probably exaggerated its significance. He looked round. It was a bright morning and the sun showed up the dust under the Lancashire chest and the carver chair. His mother had acquired both these pieces in her native county and over the years he and Mary had bought more antique furniture. The room was always described as "sitting room", and he recalled how, when they had mentioned the name they used for it to a neighbour's young child, she had asked wonderingly, 'Has it got a lot of chairs then?' He smiled at the recollection. Someone had said after the death of a partner one should not rush into change and the place remained much as it had been for years. The name "lounge" for this room might be a change he could make; it was the one he used most. He gazed at the oil painting of Ullswater and Helvellyn over the fireplace. It recalled their honeymoon, although they did not buy it then, but on a return trip to The Lakes, when they had more money for such extravagancies. Much of the furnishing was from his parents' days, although he and Mary had made changes. At the moment he could not bear to throw anything away, yet if he were to move… that awful word "downsize" as some had suggested. The clock which sat on the chest struck ten. He smiled. It had been a wedding present to Great Uncle George who had married Margaret… he had forgotten her maiden name. The present was from the employees of J. Darlington and Sons in 1912. George had died in the 1930s, but Maggie, as she was always known, lived on into the 1950s; a rather grim lady, always dressed in long black clothes, he recalled. George and Maggie had no children, and their effects were shared by the surviving members of the Darlington family, who were scattered around the country. Neither his father nor the other men of that generation had wanted to enter the family business, which was a chain of pharmacy shops, although the redoubtable Auntie Maggie kept the branch in the village going, with the help of a succession of qualified pharmacists. His mother had hated the chiming; she said it kept her awake and she had it silenced. Many years later, Nigel had found a clocksmith in a neighbouring town and had it repaired so that once again it struck, the hours and the half hours.

'Let's keep Georgie and Mags going!' he had suggested. Steven had begun to think that his mother was right. The chimes did not keep him awake but they were rather tedious. They seemed somehow ominous in their remorseless chiming. 'I do need to get away,' he said aloud to the empty house.

His neighbour, Susan Jamieson, was rather nosy but motivated by a genuine concern for his welfare. 'Do you think you'd be better in one of those new bungalows down near the playing fields? Now there's only you and with memories of Mary in every room. Make a new start while you can. I'll give you a hand with the move.' It was a sensible suggestion, but it is not always best to be sensible.

He had had other visitors; some were people he knew from church and other places in the area, they knew about Mary's death and came to offer condolences; some were clearly eyeing up the possibility of buying *Green Haugh*, although they never quite made an offer, merely hinting. 'Nice place you've got here.' He nodded, many he did not invite in.

He hadn't told his sons the other possible reason for visiting Cleadonbridge. One of his ramblings through the internet was following a visit to the churchyard and his wife's grave on the first anniversary of her death. The grave had settled, and the memorial stone was fully in place. It was a simple sandstone slab with her name and dates, *Mary Darlington 1943 – 2010*. Her last few months had been agonising and it had been difficult for him to continue his life. He found his faith severely tested, but he was supported by the boys who took long periods of leave. There were many in the village that had helped, including Susan and, of course, the Vicar. When the end came it seemed as though the whole village had crowded into the parish church on that bright but chilly March day. He nearly broke down as the coffin was brought in and the familiar words were used: *We brought nothing into the world, and we take nothing out. The Lord gave, and the Lord has taken away; blessed be the name of the Lord.*

It was impossible for him to assent to the latter part.

He did not often visit Mary's grave. His father had died before his mother and on the chilly day of the funeral as the coffin was carried up the graveyard to the burial plot, his mother had spoken.

'Steven, you remember those dreadful old green corduroy trousers he used to wear around the house and garden?'

'Yes.' He could not imagine the relevance of this.

'I threw them into the dustbin this morning. Now what's in there,' she pointed to the coffin, 'is not your father, it's just a worn out pair of trousers. He is in a better place now,' she added firmly.

Whilst agreeing with this, he did visit the grave from time to time, telling himself that it was just checking that all was as it should be. He smiled wryly as he recalled a supposed quotation from a parish magazine somewhere. "Parishioners are requested to keep their own graves tidy." He gazed around. What an enormous waste it might seem to be. Several acres of land that might otherwise have been used for production; all those monuments, which were quite expensive and which no one would look at after a few years. Yet he knew it was all very important to some parishioners.

It was a bright spring morning and very still. There were a few daffodils coming into flower and a solitary early bumble bee was inspecting them. Its buzzing was quite loud… what was that poem about a bee loud glade? Of course that was when there were lots of them.

On his return to the house he switched on the computer. It was really rather lazy to search on the internet to find the poem instead of using books but as he had no idea which book to search, this it was quicker; and the search brought up *The Lake Isle of Inisfree*, with the lines:

> *Nine bean-rows will I have there, a hive for the honey-bee,*
> *And live alone in the bee-loud glade.*

Yeats, William Butler, of course – what else did he write? He scrolled down several poems then found:

Sailing to Byzantium

> *That is no country for old men. The young*
> *In one another's arms, birds in the trees,*
> *—Those dying generations—at their song,*
> *The salmon-falls, the mackerel-crowded seas,*
> *Fish, flesh, or fowl, commend all summer long*
> *Whatever is begotten, born, and dies.*
> *Caught in that sensual music all neglect*
> *Monuments of unageing intellect.*

No country for old men, then. He chuckled. Like me. That letter from Frank Moss about the reunion, he's an old man too, as are all those who were at Cleadonbridge in the early '60s. Is that city no country for old men? *Monuments of unageing intellect.* Could that be the university? He giggled. Reading further on another line struck him. *O sages standing in God's holy fire, As in the gold mosaic of a wall.* That might be dear old St Columba's at Evensong and Benediction. He remembered that last day he was there, then searched further to find the church website. He thought about the city he had known so well for those three years. He looked at various places and then found the website of *The Kirkgate*, the theatre in Cleadonbridge. A name from the past jumped out, a name he had, he supposed, put from his mind when he left Cleadonbridge for good. He had written:

Dear Anna Ashworth,

 Your name is sufficiently unusual, especially combined with your being in Cleadonbridge and at The Kirkgate, to make it possible that we may have met, many more years ago than perhaps either of us cares to recall. I attended St. Columba's whilst a student in the town and there was a person of that name in the regular congregation. She was a young actress (or must one say "actor" these days?) and the last time I saw her was at a meeting of the discussion group which met monthly and was called, I seem to recall, The Pusey Society. You, if it was indeed you, announced just before the meeting that you had a job at a seaside rep. I cannot recall where. I gave you a congratulatory kiss in the entrance hall of the Vicarage, which caused some scandal!

 I was to have returned to Cleadonbridge in the autumn term, but I decided to take my post graduate education course at Bristol University, which was nearer my home

*in Devon, and I never returned. Forgive this intrusion,
but it might be pleasant to renew our acquaintance.*

> *With every good wish,*
> *Steven (Darlington)*

He had received a reply almost by return.

Darling Steven,

> *How well I remember that stolen kiss before the shocked
ladies of the parish! You were so handsome, and I did hope
that you might have taken things a little further. I expect
you're old and grey now, but then I'm also a little the worse
for the years. I did the summer season at Southsea (how
wonderfully alliterative!) which helped me to get my Equity
card, then returned, expecting to find you. I was so sad.*

> *Do give me a ring when you're in Cleadonbridge. As
you might imagine Mummy and Daddy died some time
ago, but they left me enough money to buy this delightful flat
quite near St. Columba's and of course, getting some work
from time to time at The Kirkgate has been wonderful.
Give me a ring when you are in town.*

She gave a landline and a mobile number.

> *I assume that as you haven't given it me you don't
have an e-mail, but here's mine in case.*

She added her e-mail address.

> *Hugs and kisses,*
> *Anna*

Steven sat for a few moments, reading the letter, and recalling the distant past. Did she and Greg make it up? Her letter had said nothing about, what was that expression some people used, a "significant other". Would any of that rather eclectic mix that was the backbone of St. Columba's congregation, be still around?

He realised that he had been day dreaming for half an hour. He roused himself and wrote a reply, deliberately not choosing to use e-mail, but "snail mail" as many now termed it. Somehow this was keeping her at arm's length, though he had already made the necessary arrangements for a trip north.

Dear Anna,

How delightful that it is you. I shall be coming to Cleadonbridge on the 26th of March and have booked a room in…

He decided not to name the B&B, nor to give his e-mail.

…a little place quite near you. My mobile phone is… We could go out for a meal; you must know a good restaurant. It would be my treat of course. I've got my lump sum, so I've got plenty of money! You write about my being old and grey; I found the following the other day when I was googling around.

That is no country for old men. The young
In one another's arms, birds in the trees,
—Those dying generations—at their song,
The salmon-falls, the mackerel-crowded seas,

Fish, flesh, or fowl, commend all summer long
Whatever is begotten, born, and dies.
Caught in that sensual music all neglect
Monuments of unageing intellect.

It's called, "Sailing to Byzantium, so it's not really
appropriate, but the first lines:

That is no country for old men. The young
In one another's arms, birds in the trees,
—Those dying generations—at their song

Are perhaps too appropriate.
With every good wish,
Steven

Her flat was in Gilbert Street, just the other side of Stanley Street and in the Georgian area of the city. It had been rather insalubrious when he was a student, but presumably it had been "gentrified". Indeed, in his trawling through entries about Cleadonbridge, he had found that it was called "The Georgian Quarter". It was nearer St. George's than St. Columba's. He smiled inwardly, recalling how they had despised them. One Sunday, walking along after Mass at St. Columba's, they had passed St. George's. The Vicar had been outside the church, chatting to some of his parishioners, his full surplice billowing in the breeze. Greg or one of the other young men made some disparaging comment about the garment. St. Columba's used the "proper" vestments.

He decided not to tell Anna about Mary's death. It would seem to be seeking sympathy and he wanted merely to revisit his old university town.

But why not have an extended stay there? It might be fun to live in a city again; the garden at *Green Haugh* was likely to become an increasing burden with the advancing years. He recalled Dr. Johnson's pronouncement, "Sir, when a man is tired of London, he is tired of life; for there is in London all that life can afford." Not that he would want to live in London, but Cleadonbridge in the twenty first century was probably about the same size as Johnson's London. He wandered over to the computer and checked that… London, it would appear was about 650,000 at the time and Cleadonbridge today was, if you took the whole conurbation, about the same.

He concluded the letter, sealed it up and decided to go to the post before he changed his mind. He had several other letters, and as he posted the one to Anna it was somehow quite satisfactory to say, aloud, 'Yes!' as the letter dropped.

'Writing in to claim a lottery prize then, Steven?' It was Susan Jamieson, whom some regarded as rather a pest, for she wanted to know everyone's business and reported it to everyone else, albeit without the exaggeration common among some gossip mongers. It would be uncharitable to think unkindly of her; she had been very supportive when Mary died.

'No Susan! I've just decided on a little trip! I need to finalise the arrangements but… will you be able to keep an eye on things?'

'Of course, just let me know when you are off. There's a lot worse thing that you can do that get out of the village and see other places. Now I was saying to Mrs. Harvey… you know her sister that lives in America has just passed on? Mind you, I did hear that she was keeping all sorts of company…' She rambled on for a while, but Steven did not listen. 'Anyway, enjoy it Steven, wherever it is! I'll keep an eye on *Green Haugh.*'

There was an implicit question in her tone and realising that she was genuinely concerned, he smiled. 'I'm going back to my old university city, Cleadonbridge, in the north! I might meet an old friend or two.'

'Your old university friends then? There'll be lots of things going on in a city like that, not that we don't have plenty happening here. As I was saying to old Mrs. Watson…'

Steven didn't really hear her, for he was planning the trip. Rail tickets he could buy at the local station, where Gary, the sole staff member, was always very helpful; he would be able to book the two sets of tickets so that he could go via Manchester and have the cheaper total fare. They were lucky to be able to do this as many stations were mere unstaffed halts. He smiled when he recalled how there had once been a stationmaster in a gold braided hat and several porters to cover the long hours that the station saw passenger trains calling. There was also a booking clerk who for some reason did not have a uniform. He could finalise his reservation for bed and breakfast on the internet. The place was on Lansdowne Terrace, which he recalled as being a wonderful Georgian development overlooking The Ravine and the city centre, with views beyond to the Pennines.

Chapter Four

Saturday 26th March 2011

On a Saturday in late March, Steven got out of the train at Cleadonbridge. The station was much as he remembered; the low roofs over the main platforms giving no anticipation of the wonderful art deco concourse. It seemed a little brighter than he remembered; the ending of steam on the railways had meant it was worth cleaning the pale stone and tile walls. He remembered his amazement when he first saw it. It was not unlike the time when he and Mary got off the train at Venice and saw the Grand Canal, with its busy procession of city traffic. Of course that was far more spectacular, but was expected; Cleadonbridge station had not been. In Venice they had simply stood there and marvelled. He now stood awhile in thought; nearly half a century ago he arrived here as a rather naïve student, fresh from a country grammar school and about to begin an adventure. His recollection was of bright sunny October weather. Today, although it was sunny, it was noticeably cooler than it had been when he boarded the train in Devon; it was drizzling and there was a nasty little wind nipping round the corners, as he discovered when he left the station. He shivered and pulled his coat more closely around him.

'This is why I didn't want to return!'

He must have spoken the words aloud, for a woman just ahead of him turned round. 'Now then, the rain's clearing and it will be sunny and warmer tomorrow, or perhaps the next day, you'll see.' She spoke with the distinctive local accent that he had almost forgotten. Sometimes he had found it almost unintelligible. He was tempted to ask her if this was based on local weather lore, information from the Met Office or was simply optimism.

'I hope so!' was his only comment as he turned his collar up and walked over to the line of buses waiting in the wide sweep of the station approach. He had a hatred of seeming to be a tourist or a stranger and was cross with himself for having uttered the earlier remark that clearly indicated that he was not a resident of the city. He might have walked the kilometre or so to Lansdowne Terrace, as he had packed everything in a rucksack, but after all, the bus was now free. He pretended to be fumbling for his bus pass, whilst looking furtively at the destinations of buses; the numbering of the routes didn't seem familiar. Presumably privatisation had changed all that. He spotted one going to Longcroft, which he recalled as being a large council overspill estate on the western fringe; he assumed that it would pass along Gilbert Street, which was parallel to Lansdowne Terrace. Showing his pass to the driver, he climbed up the stairs and within a minute the bus set off. At the top of King William Street he was annoyed to find the bus swinging right instead of continuing up the hill. Two stops further along he got out and made his way through The Ravine to Lansdowne Terrace. There was a climb up from the park to reach the nineteenth century middle class suburb at the top. It had not occurred to him before, but this conversion of the quarries after their closure was probably because of their being adjacent to the first middle class suburb of Cleadonbridge. Had access been limited to the well to do who lived in places such as Gilbert Street? On a whim, he had used a family history website to discover who lived in the house where Anna now lived. He found that in 1871 it was the home of a wine merchant and his family who had a servant. Perhaps servants would have been permitted to wander here, and of course the nannies would have wheeled their charges into the gardens. Would some of them have attended St Columba's? As he walked up the gently sloping road from the former quarries, built in the eighteenth century to allow carts to bring the stone out; he imagined that in the nineteenth century, after its transformation, the nannies would push prams up its slope which led to Stanley Street. From here he was able to saunter along to his B&B. Catching the wrong bus had meant that he would not have to pass where Anna lived on Gilbert Street. He wanted to have time to himself first.

The area seemed to have a much less seedy and run down appearance than it had fifty years ago and was more like "The Bloomsbury of Cleadonbridge" as someone had called it. It had been teetering on the edge of being a slum when he was a student. The stone built three storey Georgian terraces of the main street were obviously divided into flats; the two storey smaller houses in the side streets might, he supposed, be in single ownership. But whereas half a century ago, the paintwork had been peeling and the window frames rotting, all was now repaired and newly painted. The houses had then been subdivided and doors were often standing open, revealing a dirty common hall and stairway. Gilbert Street was in the area of bigger houses he recalled. He returned to his thoughts on Doctor Johnson's comments about living in London and his own comparison with the size of London then and Cleadonbridge today. Theatres, art galleries, concerts were all much more available than in Exeter and he could walk to them if he lived here. And as long as he remained able to stride out over the hills, there was glorious north country walking.

The Osborne, the bed and breakfast that he had found, was one of the grander houses. Lansdowne Terrace ran along the side of The Ravine so the houses must have been at a premium. In Victorian times this household was also headed by a merchant, but they had four servants and a governess for the children. The doorbell was answered within seconds by a small, quiet lady of perhaps fifty who showed him to his spotlessly clean room on the third floor, which had, as he had requested, a view over The Ravine. He unpacked, had a shower, then sat down and gazed out on the familiar yet unfamiliar townscape. As it had stopped raining, he decided to take a stroll and look at the area he had once known so well. He walked to St. Columba's, but the door was firmly barred. Fifty years ago it had been possible to keep the church open during the day. He smiled ruefully as he remembered the day when the kids rushing in and out of the church had been scolded by Greg.

He recalled his first Sunday when, with Greg, he had made his way there for the 11 o'clock High Mass. Only familiar with the limited ceremonial of his home church, he was somewhat bewildered and followed the lead of the other worshippers as to when he should stand, kneel, bow and cross himself. Greg was in the sanctuary, serving as… was it thurifer, making huge clouds of incense? Before the end of that first term he too was assisting at the altar. In spite of his being rather uncertain of what to do that first time, he had felt somehow uplifted. Yet he wondered if in reality it was some sort of act of defiance. He chuckled when he thought how he had pointedly said to his mother in a telephone call that he had been to the 11 o'clock High Mass. Was it just adolescent rebellion, albeit of a very mild sort, or was he seeking something? Was the ritual spiritually uplifting, as he always claimed? Greg had grown up in the Anglo-Catholic tradition, so it had none of the illicit thrill it had brought to Steven. He had no idea where Greg was now, or even if he were still alive. They had kept up a rather desultory correspondence for a few years and then Steven's last letter was not answered. He assumed that Greg had decided to end their friendship. He wondered if he had been frightened of him. Certainly he had seemed to dominate his life, at least those parts of it which overlapped with Greg's.

Beyond St.Columba's stretched the Boulevard; he set off along it towards the University. The houses here, Victorian in age rather than Georgian, seemed more run down than in Lansdowne Terrace, but they were in better repair than he remembered them. Behind the gracious four storey terraces had been close packed, small terrace houses. These must have been demolished as there were now flats and maisonettes, as he believed they were termed; he guessed they were late 1960's in age; the redevelopment must have taken place after he had left Cleadonbridge.

Some of the incidents of half a century ago came back. He smiled at the recollection of their all sitting around until the small hours… who was it who in final year had a flat hereabouts? They had chatted about the affairs of the world, so sure that they knew the answers to everything. They had argued about religion too, one of the others who shared that flat was a fundamentalist; the other two were atheists. It had been a fascinating debate and he felt he might have convinced one of the two atheists… certainly that there was an explanation other than taking the literal words of the Bible. His thoughts about the religious argument brought him to the present day for he was approaching St Peter's, in a commanding position at the end of the Boulevard. He recalled that it was a very typical "low" church. He wandered down and whilst still some distance from it he could see a banner stretched across the west front of the church: *You are Redeemed by Jesus.* They might be fundamentalists too, though the guy in that flat all those years ago was a member of a small free church. He passed the building and went into the University Precinct, as they had termed it in those days. He smiled wryly as he saw a map which described it as "Campus". Creeping Americanisms – who was it has been complaining about that the other day? But so many new buildings had been added he felt quite lost, so he decided to leave it for another day.

He then returned to *The Osborne* and telephoned Anna. She had given him both her mobile phone and her landline; absurdly, he thought that like most young people, she would have her mobile with her and switched on at all times. He laughed out loud, for in his mind he was telephoning a pretty young woman of about nineteen. He was still chuckling when the answer phone message crackled in.

'This is Anna, busy as always. I can't take your call now; leave a message and I'll try to get back…'

The voice was not that of an old woman; it sounded almost like the Anna he remembered. He was wondering whether to try the landline when Anna herself broke in.

'Hello?'

'It's Steven, Steven Darlington, you remember, we…'

'Steven darling! Where are you?' She giggled. 'Darling, Darlington…'

'Only round the corner, as it happens. *The Osborne* on Lansdowne Terrace.'

'Oh, that's wonderful! Can you come round here now?'

'I think so, if that's all right?'

'Of course it's all right! After all you came up to Cleadonbridge just to see me, didn't you?' Her tone was almost seductive, and Steven again was imagining a young girl almost pouting.

'Well…' He felt himself blushing. 'I wanted to see the old place again and…'

'I'm only joking Steven dear!'

In a few moments he was ringing the bell; it was one of half a dozen at the side of the portico. Anna opened it almost immediately; she must have been waiting.

'Steven!' She opened her arms and he allowed her to envelop him. It was only recently that an embrace, even a kiss, had become commonplace among people who were not, as one might say, lovers. But such kisses were the mere brushing of the cheek; Anna's kiss was on the mouth.

She seemed about to explore further. He pulled away, embarrassed. To show that he was not totally rejecting her, he placed a kiss on the top of her head.

'It's lovely to see you too.' He looked at her closely for the first time. She was a few years younger than he was, so she must be in her late sixties. Her hair was, as he remembered it, blonde; it was quite long and tied back. Presumably she had to be able to create whatever hair style suited the role she was taking, and this would give some flexibility. She had a pair of jeans in a softer tone and material than most wore, and a sort of 'homespun' top. She wore a necklace of what appeared to be beans. He supposed that he must describe her as "well preserved", a horrible phrase. Since Mary's death he had admired pretty women from afar. Much as one would admire paintings he had thought, perhaps the Mona Lisa, but he had never… What was that phrase from the Bible? *But I say unto you, that whosoever looks on a woman to lust after her has committed adultery with her already in his heart.* Not that he really believed that it was so terrible to lust after a woman; at least as long as it was consensual sex that one sought. He'd just not been interested in sex and… Was he now? Anna's apparent advance had not seemed to do anything for him. Was he perhaps too old for it? Although these thoughts passed through his mind, he merely said, 'Now you promised me tea.'

'Of course. A real afternoon tea with scones, jam and cream.'

Was she a little put out? Her expression suggested disappointment, but she smiled and led the way upstairs. She had indeed secured a delightful flat. Most of the first floor, the piano nobile, had been converted and its large windows overlooked the busy street and gave a glimpse of the trees in The Ravine. The room was huge, as they were in those days of gracious living, and he wondered how easy it was to heat; it seemed rather chilly on this damp day.

Anna noticed his shiver. 'Is someone walking over your grave Steven? Or are you just feeling the cold? This place can be a bit like an ice box in winter and we aren't allowed to light a fire, though that grate is simply asking to be used.' She pointed to an Adam style fireplace, which he assumed was original. The plasterwork ceiling surely was.

'It is a bit on the chill side, but don't worry. This area has certainly changed for the better since I first knew it.'

'I don't think I'd have wanted to live here as it was. Mummy was very keen to remain involved in the life of a slum parish, as she described it, but she would no more have dreamed of living here than going to the Moon.'

He marvelled at the almost childish use of the word "Mummy", which seemed to be at odds with her self assured manner. 'I assumed that she was attracted to St. Columba's high church ritual.' He laughed. 'I was. It was a sort of rebellion against my parents. Do you still go to St. Columba's?'

She hesitated. 'Not so as you'd notice it.'

'I thought I'd go on Sunday.'

'It won't be as you remember.'

'How do you know if you don't go?'

'I go once or twice a year for auld lang syne. But there will be only a handful there, in the chancel or the Lady Chapel. Father Tom does his best, but there's no choir and only one server, not the full complement that you were once part of.'

'It said on the website, Family Friendly, Coffee and Incense".'

'Well I suppose it will be all of that.'

'Will you come?'

'I won't promise. There's only the 10.30 now you know – the High Mass that there used to be at 11.00 was combined with the earlier and plainer celebration, the old Parish Mass. That started the rot really. There's no Early Mass either.'

'The rot?'

'Well people like Mummy wanted the smells and bells and when that was toned down, they stopped coming. In any case it wasn't really daring anymore.'

'I suppose it was a bit daring to go to St. Columba's.'

'It was almost illegal. The bishops in the nineteenth and early twentieth centuries got frightfully cross about high church practices. They saw 'ritualism' as they termed it, as an attempt to destroy the Protestant basis of the Church of England and bring it closer to Rome in doctrine and practice. So for some, like Mummy, there was a sort of illicit thrill. Then after the war, when the area went downhill, you had the added buzz of slumming it, at least for an hour on Sunday, after which you went back to the comfortable middle class ambience of Park Crescent. But others of the old families continued to come!'

'Like the Walmsleys, you mean?'

'Yes, and the Hallworths. Their memories went back to the days when the whole area was still one of gracious living and servants. That was why there was the 10.00 Mass, for servants and of course the few who came from the streets of smaller terraced houses.'

'We still had some of those in my day.'

'Anyway, tea!' She disappeared to the kitchen, returning a few minutes later with a tray, including some scones, and dishes containing jam and whipped cream. 'All home made! The kettle's boiled I'll bring the tea.' As she entered bearing the tea tray she asked, 'Are you married, or anything?'

'I was…' Did he imagine it, or was there a hopeful look? 'Mary and I were married for over forty years, but she died last year.'

'I'm so sorry.' She seemed genuinely concerned. 'What…?'

'Cancer. In the end it was peaceful, but…' His voice tailed away. 'But we had a wonderful funeral. Half the village turned out.'

'All the holy smoke and water?'

'Hardly – it's a small and conservative west country parish.'

She smiled. 'And did you have children?'

He told her about Nigel in Melbourne and Paul in Auckland, Sandra, and the twin boys.

'You were in teaching I think you said?'

'I taught geography. For a while I was in a boys' grammar school in Bristol; Mary was at the sister school. We met because we organised a joint walking group. After my parents died in fairly quick succession in the late '70s I inherited the house, I was an only child so it all came to me.'

'That's *Green Haugh*?'

He nodded. 'We had the kids by then and Mary had retired for the time being and I got a job nearby in the local college of FE.'

'FE?'

'Further Education. I retired from that a few years back now. And you; are you married?' He wasn't sure if he wanted her to be free.

'No. I was married for a few years to a bit of a wastrel, a fellow actor called Will. We never had kids; there didn't seem time somehow. We parted by mutual consent, years ago. Technically we are still married. We send each other Christmas and birthday cards and if we happen to find ourselves in the same town, we may have lunch and a natter. There's no animosity, but no love either. I'm not sure if there ever was any actually.'

He felt helpless. 'I'm sorry,' he stammered. 'Did you ever get together again with Greg?'

'No. He dumped me after he graduated, went off to London and when he came home at weekends and so on, he would wave cheerfully and shout "Hi!" but no more. I avoided him when I could. And then…' She paused.

'Then?'

'He was killed.'

'Killed?'

'In a car crash. You know how he always went hell for leather for everything, took charge and…'

'Yes.'

'Well he had a car and was driving with some friends. They were in the country, I forget where… somewhere in Surrey, I think, and it was said that he was well over the limit. The car was wrapped round a tree at the side of the road. They were all killed instantly. He had a wonderful funeral here at St. Columba's.' There was a catch in her voice as she spoke these last words.

'When was this, Greg's death, I mean?' he asked.

'The 17th of March, St Patrick's Day, in 1965. He had an Irish girlfriend and a whole gang of them decided to celebrate at a country pub he knew.'

There was an uncomfortable silence; Steven realised that it had affected Anna deeply and indeed it still was causing her some distress. 'It was about that time I think that he stopped replying to my letters, but nobody told me he had died.'

'Well, Steven darling,' she said and beamed brightly, 'if you had kept in touch with me I would have told you and... well, who knows?'

Again he speculated on his feelings all those years ago; his not writing was perhaps his fear of an emotional entanglement with her, so recently spurned by Greg, who might have turned really nasty; it was easier to flee Cleadonbridge and do the post graduate education course in Bristol.

He remembered Michelle, a girl he'd taken out a few times when he was a student; she had made it clear that she wanted to have sex with him. They had coffee in his room in hall and she had lain on the bed in an inviting manner; he resisted... resisted what? Temptation? He had never known if Anna and Greg had "gone all the way" as it was described in those days, but he thought perhaps that they had. Although there was the remark of Greg's about Cleadonbridge not being wicked enough... Steven had wondered what he had meant by that. Was it that in London he could have full sexual licence that was denied here? Did he bed the Irish maiden? He imagined her as a temptress with flaming red hair and green eyes.

'You quoted that poem. *That is no country for old men.*'
Her voice tailed away. 'I looked it up and it seems that Yeats
wrote it because felt this was no place for him, so as death
approached he went away. I think that's what it's about.'
She sighed deeply. 'Or no country for…' She paused

Was Anna about to add "us", assuming his intention
was… But this was ridiculous. Had she thought it? He was
embarrassed at the recollection. He had not intended that
this was not a place for him and her; he had not thought in
detail about the poem's meaning.

'I copied a bit of *Sailing to Byzantium*. You had a
wonderful voice as I remember. Will you read some poetry
to me now?'

'Well, I…'

'Not Yeats. And you are not an old man; you are in
the prime of life.' She stood up and planted a kiss on his
head as she moved to the bookshelves and pulled down a
volume. 'What about this?' She smiled enigmatically.

He took the book and read the selected work by
Betjeman about the old days of High Church assemblies.

'I remembered rightly. You do have a beautiful voice.
You should have joined CUDS with Greg. Why didn't you?'

'I didn't think I was up to it. Greg was a good actor
though.'

'Perhaps not as good as you.' She raised her eyebrows
archly. 'You might even have considered a career on the
stage.'

'I do a bit of Am Dram in the village. I only became
involved when we moved there after my parents died.'

'I'll bet you're very good.' She leaned forward and
placed her hand on his knee.

He drew away slightly. 'When my mother was ill during the war and with Dad in the army, we got a lady from the village to come and look after us, Miss Banks. My mother told me that Miss Banks once said, after I staged one of those temper tantrums as kids of that age do, "If that child doesn't go on the stage, it'll be great loss to the acting profession".'

'And that was a pretty fair attempt at a Mummersetshire accent my dear!'

'I wanted a secure job with a pension,' he protested.

'Well I haven't that, certainly. But I have had, still have, the most marvellous job in the world.'

'Acting?'

'Of course. Did you not enjoy teaching?'

'Yes, I did, and there were sometimes great rewards but how...'

'I love the thrill, the rush of adrenalin I guess it is, before you go on stage and it's a safer way of getting it that going on the hills, like you do, where you might break a bone or worse.'

Steven protested. 'I've never had a serious accident on the hills and I don't really get an adrenalin rush... although I suppose that time when we came down the wrong way off a Munroe in the Highlands in mist and we were hanging on by our eyebrows... what the hell was its name... I think it was a Ben More, but there are dozens of those.'

Anna's eyebrows were raised. 'A Munroe? As in Marilyn?'

Steven smiled. 'The Munros are the mountains in Scotland over 3000 feet high, or 914 metres if you prefer it.'

'I'll stick with feet. How many are there and why "Munros"?'

'There are over two hundred and they were listed by a chappie called Sir Hugh Munro in the late nineteenth century, hence the name.'

'Have you done them all?'

'Nowhere near all of them – perhaps about fifty; I have some friends who have. But it's a great thrill when you bag another peak and you are sitting on top of the world.'

Anna was silent for a moment. 'It is then for you, perhaps a bit like being in the theatre when you realise that you've somehow connected with the other actors and the audience and… you share something, something you cannot find elsewhere. It's magical.'

'I don't think I've ever felt like that about acting. I can do it, but…' He paused. 'Other things took precedence.'

'I suppose for me everything was subordinated to it. But I didn't ask you to read that simply to let me hear your public speaking ability.'

'No?' He realised he was almost being coy in his utterance of the monosyllable, and it was Anna's turn to be the one to rebuff.

'Don't you see? This,' she said and pointed to the book, 'is chuntering on about Anglo-Catholics, when they were running counter to the Establishment; it was exciting, risqué. But all bishops wear copes now; many churches have eucharistic vestments. Even… Do you know that the image of Our Lady of Walsingham was taken to the Cathedral last year? The Dean said it was of major importance and that it's of a tradition of churchmanship that contributes enormously to the Church of England. Can you imagine that having happened in your day in Cleadonbridge? They carried the image in, and we were all sprinkled with holy water.'

'You went?'

'Yes, it was a sort of duty for Mummy. She loved Walsingham.'

Steven chuckled. 'I remember how she was always trying to persuade everyone to go to Walsingham.'

Anna giggled. 'That's just how she pronounced it, in a sort of strangled way, with the emphasis on the last syllable. Your Miss Banks was right! You could have been an actor if you wanted to enough.'

'Yes, well.' He felt quite baffled at the various twists and turns of the conversation.

'You haven't finished your scone!' She spoke almost accusingly.

He felt somewhat guilty. 'I couldn't read with my mouth full! Sorry; they are delicious. Home made you said?'

'Yes, and the jam, Mummy's recipes.'

There was a rather uncomfortable silence. Steven wasn't quite sure what was the reason for the discomfort.

'Those were the battles of yesteryear, and they were won by the Anglo Catholics; their patterns of worship are the norm, the standard now.'

'I suppose so.'

'But the despised "Protestants" as we used to say, Betjeman uses the term there, are growing. In the old days there was only one main morning service at St. Peter's, Matins, now there are two, 9 o'clock and 11.00, whilst there is only the 10.30 at St Columba's. It's all very happy-clappy at Pete's, as they call it, but it pulls them in, partly because John Coleman is a bit of a charismatic figure.'

'You seem to know thing pretty well; you must have been then?'

'I'm curious.'

'What about St. George's?'

'That struggles, like St Columba's.'

'Come with me tomorrow to St Columba's?'

'I'll see.'

'I'll meet you there?'

He left shortly afterwards and as he wandered along the street to his B&B he thought again about the reason for his visit. He had wanted to meet Anna, but did he want to bed her? For many people nowadays sex seemed much freer; freer of emotional complications and consequences. He was struck with the horrible tortured thought that he had wanted a full relationship with Anna all those years go, had fled from the complications and that in reality Mary had been but second best. This was nonsense. He had forgotten about Anna by the time he met Mary over six years later. No, he had made the decision to shake the dust of this town off his feet. And yet he had returned. He pondered the words of the poem by Yeats which kept coming back. *That is no country for old men.*

Chapter Five

Sunday 27th March 2011

He had risen early on the following morning, which was Sunday, hoping to meet Anna at St Columba's for the 10.30 Parish Mass. As he approached he saw Anna turn the corner and they met on the steps. It was 10.25, but he had seen only a couple of people enter ahead of him and there was no one else heading towards the church. Suddenly the small cracked bell in the tiny turret was tugged rapidly and its somewhat strangled summons seemed to have had an effect as two more could be seen advancing in that purposeful yet unhurried way that denotes a churchgoer. Behind them a middle age black lady scurried along, looking at her watch. Half a century earlier, at a little short of 11.00, there would have been quite a number on the pavement outside the church as the congregation from the 10.00 celebration left, meeting the ones attending the 11.00 High Mass. The earlier worshippers were from the working class streets on either side of the Boulevard. There were not very many, but some of those who had attended the parish school which had a weekly service in church had continued to attend services after they had left the school. Those at the 11.00 service were for the most part older and were fairly well-to-do middle class. There was no real distinction in their dress or the manner of their greeting each other. In his student days whilst on a camping holiday in the West of Ireland he had gone to Morning Service in the Anglican church in the little town and had observed a real distinction between those who sat on the front rows, who were dressed in tweeds; he had assumed that they were of the minor gentry. After the final blessing, they moved out graciously acknowledging the deference shown to them by those who occupied the back pews. These were clad in "Sunday Best", the men's suits almost threadbare with age and the material shiny. Their deference did not quite include tugging of forelocks or curtseys, but there were some slight gestures of that type. However, although the differences in wealth and social class in the two congregations at St. Columba's mirrored those in that Irish church, no such distinctions of dress or manners had been evident here.

Hearing the bell also brought back memories of arriving on days when there was a major festival and the cathedral bells were rung, their booming seemed an almost calculated insult to St. Columba's. A sort of apartheid existed between the Cathedral and St. Columba's. Some of the bishops had fulminated against the high church practices, but under the curious system of the parson's freehold and patronage, the bishop could not remove the Vicar. The patron was a college with impeccably high church principles and ensured that its appointee held such views.

'Hello!' Anna's greeting was somewhat less effusive than it had been yesterday. No kiss was offered.

'Hi! Glad you were able to make it. Shall we go in?'

A black man, who seemed somehow familiar, emerged

from the church, waving to the lady who had almost reached the steps.

'Sorted?' he asked her. She nodded breathlessly. He turned to Steven and Anna. 'So you're going to join us today?' Steven was surprised; he expected an African or Caribbean accent and the man spoke with the local accent.

'Yes. We both are.' He turned to Anna for confirmation of this.

'Well you're a long time member Anna,' said the lady. 'Nice that you are bringing a friend.' She turned to Steven. 'I'm Sue Edwards by the way. And this is Denny, my husband; he's one of the churchwardens.' She spoke with evident pride.

'Denny Edwards. Don't you remember him?' Anna asked. Steven realised now who he was. 'Yes, it's him, Steven. You were a bit of a tearaway then weren't you, Denny?' Anna's tone was almost patronising, but the churchwarden didn't seem to resent it. 'This is Steven – he was here a long time ago, one of that little band of students.'

'I think I can remember, but we'd better go in.' He held the door open and motioned them to enter.

The young man he had seen in the distance had now arrived and hovered uneasily at the bottom of the steps, smiled nervously, and followed them in. One or two others were also arriving.

Altogether there might have been twenty five worshippers in a church that was designed to hold at least two hundred; all were in the choir stalls, where the lighting was switched on. This, with daylight streaming through the large east window and the candles on the altar created a feeling of light and warmth, which contrasted with the empty gloominess of the nave; some reflections of the chancel lights caused the gilded wall paintings to twinkle and this seemed to emphasise the emptiness. Yet as he looked beyond the altar to the east window he was transported, not just back to his youth, but somehow elevated above the humdrum, a view of heaven perhaps. The sacristy bell tinkled. It awoke further memories in Steven's mind, and he expected to see crucifer, thurifer and boat boy, acolytes MC… What was the order they arrived? Finally would be the Celebrant, Deacon and Sub Deacon, all clad in sumptuous vestments. Today there were only three, the first was a small boy carrying a cross which seemed too big for him; it looked as though he might drop it.

'That's my grandson, Benjy!' whispered Sue who was sitting behind.

Benjy was followed by a somewhat rotund man carrying a thurible and finally by Father Tom, clad in a purple chasuble which was certainly sumptuous, but one which had seen better days.

The service followed the order of the new Common Worship, rather than the Prayer Book which he had expected; he had hoped for the once familiar, yet now unfamiliar words of Cranmer, though why he should want such he could not imagine; his own parish church had adopted Common Worship from the beginning. He thought it must be that it was because he wanted to go back fifty years and start again from there; he told himself not to be so silly.

The tattered copies of *The English Hymnal* seemed to have been the ones they had used half a century before and for such a tiny number, the singing, accompanied by a lady on a harmonium, was lusty. The grand pipe organ was no longer in working order he guessed. The old Lenten favourites were there; the first one they sang was number 73:

> *Forty days and forty nights,*
> *Thou wast fasting in the wild.*

He was amused to see 72, the "prowling hymn" as his father had termed it.

> *Christian, Dost Thou See Them*
> *On the holy ground*
> *How the troops of Midian*
> *Prowl and prowl around…*

He turned on further – here it was, 107. "You can always remember my house, hymn number one oh seven, *When I Survey the Wondrous Cross.*" What was that old lady's name? She lived in St. Columba's parish and he had given her a hand with her shopping.

The chubby middle aged server, whom he thought he recognised, swung the thurible with enthusiasm and Steven found himself almost choking. He remembered that one gave a little bow to acknowledge the censing; how easily it all came back. Father Tom's sermon was short and to the point. He managed to involve the four children of primary school age, explaining how Jesus wants us to be happy and to be his faithful soldiers and servants, using various bits and bobs of things he produced from the pocket of his cassock. Turning then to the adults and using the Psalm appointed for the day, he urged them also to be happy.

O come, let us sing to the Lord;
let us heartily rejoice in the rock of our salvation.
Let us come into his presence with thanksgiving
and be glad in him with psalms.

Steven remembered this in the Prayer Book form, sung at Matins, and was transported back to his youth, back to the village church in Devon. The teacher in him delighted in Father Tom's communication skills. He rejoiced too that it was short as there was no heating in the church and he was beginning to feel very cold. By 11.20 they were filing through into the Vicarage for coffee and biscuits. 'There's no parish school now. The building was condemned and demolished years ago,' Anna explained. 'They have to use the Vicarage.'

'Serving coffee after services is something that came in later. Most churches do now, but I don't think anyone did in the days when I was a student here. But there was a Sunday School there – run by the nuns. I didn't know we had nuns in the C of E until that first Sunday and two of them appeared and escorted the kids out.'

'Sadly, that's another thing that's gone – numbers in the convent had dwindled so much that they closed it, twenty or so years ago. Mummy was still alive, and she was so sad.' Anna giggled. 'I think she hoped I might become a nun.'

As they moved out, Steven said to Anna, 'I'm wondering if I've grown out of the holy smoke and water. That guy with the thurible was a bit over enthusiastic.'

She smiled. 'Didn't you recognise him? It was Jim Dewhurst?'

'No! He's put on a bit of weight.'

'He likes his food too much; he eats rather too many takeaways I suspect.'

'There are special biscuits and cake too!' a large and jolly lady told them. 'It's our Golden Wedding!' She pointed out her husband, a rather thin man, who looked somewhat ill at ease.

'Were you married here?' Steven asked politely.

'Oh yes. Father Mainwaring took the service.'

'Of course, he was here when I was a student.'

They chatted about the affairs of half a century earlier; she had been one of those who went to the 10.00 service, but they knew some people in common. He learned that most had died or moved away.

'I'm afraid there's just such a little few of us now. I mean,' she indicated her husband, 'he never goes. I had to twist his arm today.'

Jim entered the room. He had changed and was wearing a suit with a rather garish bow tie.

Anna went up to him. 'Jim here's an old friend.'

The chubby man peered at Steven, adjusted his glasses, and bent forward. 'How many guesses have I got, Anna? I'm sorry, dear sir, but I cannot for the life of me place you.' His voice was rather fruity; Steven would have recognised that, although the face and the figure had changed.

He held out his hand. 'Steven Darlington.'

'Good heavens! It must be half a century or more since you were here, in tandem with that jackanapes, Greg. Sorry Anna; I know you and he had fling.'

'It was more than a mere fling, Jim, but don't worry, I'm over it now.'

'So, is this your latest beau?'

'No! Jim. We are just good friends.'

'That's what they always say!' He dug Steven in the ribs. 'But somebody said that there's cake today.' He rubbed his hands in cheerful anticipation.

'Is Martin Barnes still around?' asked Steven to change the subject. He recalled him as a tall, rather good-looking man of part African descent.

'He married a girl from Melcester and they moved there years ago. He's a granddad now and his wife seduced him.'

'Seduced him?'

'There was no Catholic church there, so they went to hers… its very "low.". I don't think they go all that often. When they visited here many years back their kids loved lighting candles and so on, he said he would try and find a Catholic church in Melcester. I don't know if he did. We've sort of lost touch.'

Steven had forgotten how Anglo-Catholics used the term "Catholic" to refer to their type of Anglicanism. 'What about Ted Harris?'

Jim chuckled. 'I'm afraid he "went over".'

"Went over?" Steven echoed. 'Oh, became RC.'

'Indeed. As someone said, "He forsook the errors of Canterbury for those of Rome.".'

But their reminiscing was cut short by the arrival of Father Tom. 'Bessie, why didn't you tell me?' he almost shouted from the door. 'We could have announced it during the Mass, given you a round of applause.' He made a little speech now and the couple got their round of applause. Her husband looked as though he might burst into tears. Father Tom moved among his flock, exchanging a few words with the shy young man who had arrived at the same time as Steven and introducing him to another member of the congregations.

He now approached them. 'Anna, nice to see you.'

'Hello Father, here's another old Columban, if we say that. Steven was a student in the 1960s!'

'And are you living in Cleadonbridge now?'

Steven explained his situation.

Father Tom nodded and expressed sorrow when Mary's death was mentioned. 'Well it's good you were able to join us. But if you'll excuse me… Denny!' He moved over to the churchwarden.

As they left Steven spoke. 'St Columba's a mere shadow of itself, as you warned me.'

'You could always try St. Cuthbert's. That's a real spike shop, smells and bells, the works. It's right out in the eastern wastelands of the city.'

'Isn't it one of the Forward in Faith churches though? I saw it when looked up to make sure St Columba's wasn't.'

'What's Forward in Faith?'

'Some call them Backward in Bigotry.' He looked quizzically at her.

'Oh, those who won't have women priests!'

'Exactly. And I have resolved not to have anything to do with them unless I have to.'

'It would seem that you are a feminist then, Steven! You certainly weren't all those years ago. You thought a woman's place was in the home.'

He felt discomfited. 'Well, we all change our views.'

'I need to get my head down this afternoon and learn lines. I don't find it as easy as I used to. 'That cake was quite adequate for lunch, for me at least.'

'Me too. I never eat much at midday.'

'The director expects us to be absolutely word perfect at rehearsal tomorrow because we open later this week, but how about our meeting this evening for dinner?'

Steven was a little embarrassed. 'In all that chat about my amateur dramatics I forgot to ask what play you are in at the moment. I'm sorry!'

'We are doing a remarkably silly play: *Death on the Mersey*! I'm…'

'The murderess?'

Anna smiled. 'No, I'm a gossip columnist on the local paper; it's quite a good part, but in any case, women of my age cannot be choosers.'

'Anyway, let's have dinner together. Have you any suggestions?'

'There's a little BYO place near me *The Riviera*, it's a sort of Mediterranean cuisine, very good and quite cheap.'

'BYO?'

'Bring your own, wine, that is.'

'I'll get a nice bottle of red wine before I come. What time shall we meet?'

'Make it 8.00. I'll give Konni a ring and book a table.'

'Connie?' He had a mental picture of a lady with grey hair drawn back into a bun and wearing steel rimmed spectacles, not quite fitting somehow with a Mediterranean restaurant.

'Not Connie as in your great aunt, but as in Konstantin.

He's Greek but has some sort of Italian and Lebanese connections. Meet me there; it's easier.' She explained where the restaurant was.

★

He hadn't been sure how to spend that Sunday afternoon, but eventually decided to go for a stroll down the Boulevard, to Belford Park and into the University Campus. As he approached St. Peter's he saw again the banner stretched across the west end of the church. *You are Redeemed by Jesus!* He moved closer; the times of the services were given, though there was no indication of the type of service. The banner was related to the Alpha Course, he observed, which was to be conducted every Wednesday in the parish hall. He knew little about Alpha but believed it to be well-organised, well-funded and so sure of its own dogma that it wears down opponents into passive submission. Why did he feel not only his usual discomfort at such an approach, but yet was strangely drawn to it? He smiled ruefully as he thought how they had despised such places. Nowadays they were thriving; what was it Anna had said? "It's all very happy-clappy, but it pulls them in, partly because John Coleman is a bit of a charismatic figure." Why should the Catholic ritual not pull them in? What could be an equivalent headline? There were images of people in various life stages and states of happiness. One struck him forcibly; it showed a group of people, with hands aloft. It was evidently a charismatic act of worship, although it reminded him also of the scenes in clubs. He chuckled at the remembrance of the boys taking him to a club in Exeter, just after Mary had died. It had started as a joke, but, because he was sure they would themselves want a little opportunity to relax, and he knew they would not want to leave him, he had persuaded them that they should all go. But for St. Columba's... what could they call it? *Bringing us all to God the Catholic Way*. No, that wouldn't do, it would be assumed it was R.C. It could be combined with an image that would suggest the quiet contemplative spirituality of the Catholic way, perhaps of a woman priest raising the chalice at a modern altar. Not "Kyrie with Lace On", as someone had rudely described the excesses of another Anglo Catholic parish where the servers wore short elaborate embroidered cottas. It would be better if it were done professionally which would need money; and after all he had some.

By now he had passed St. Peter's, entered the park and paused in his reverie. It was nearly spring and he took an almost childish pleasure in looking for the signs of the new season. The sun was starting to come out, and some of the early shrubs were in bloom. One he thought was probably a viburnum. There were other trees all about to come into leaf and he spotted a bird but he wasn't sure which species. Was it a nuthatch? He then returned to the theme of reviving St Columba's. Money could do a lot; he had a lot of money, or he could have if he sold *Green Haugh*. After all, he didn't need all the space and the garden was a bit tying. Living in the city he could have access to the parks with their wealth of flowers... Why not buy a nice flat like Anna's, perhaps quite near her. How much would they cost?

He abandoned the idea of going on to the University and on the spur of the moment walked briskly to the nearest exit from the park and waited for a bus into the city centre instead. Having a bus pass meant that this didn't cost him anything and although the walk would be beneficial, he would have more time in town. He got off in the centre and after a little trouble found an estate agent. He scanned the window, eventually spotting one that was near Anna's, but in a side street, which meant that the house was quite small compared with the one which included her flat. However, this was a whole house offered for sale.

£295,000. An opportunity for a cash buyer to purchase a large town house, situated in a prime location. The property is a listed building and, as such, will need care and attention to restore it to its former glory. The accommodation comprises: Spacious ground floor reception rooms, cellar, drawing room to the first floor and four bedrooms set over two floors. To the rear there are gardens.

Green Haugh would fetch at least double that, leaving him with enough to move and to do this place up. A bit of garden, so his horticultural enthusiasm could find an outlet. That size would mean he could take in lodgers; it could be quite a good investment. The photo of the first floor drawing room suggested something quite gracious, and he could already imagine filling it with his parents' antique furniture together with those pieces that he and Mary had collected over the years. He glanced at his watch; there was plenty of time to go and have a look at the place before it got dark. Although the agent was open, he didn't yet want to commit himself even to that extent. If there was one like this there would be others. But a flat might be better as there wouldn't be costs and worry. Here was one.

> *£97,950. Two bedroom flat for sale. Affording wonderful views and located close to the fashionable Georgian Quarter yet within easy reach of the city centre, this top floor apartment is being offered with no onward chain. Briefly comprising: Communal secure entry, reception hall, 17 foot lounge, fitted kitchen, two double bedrooms and bathroom in addition to double glazing and allocated secure parking.*

Now that would have advantages, though he wasn't sure he would want to run a car if he lived in the city centre. He'd go and look at both of them.

This time he found the correct bus out of the city centre, got off a few stops short and, taking a slightly devious route to avoid passing Anna's flat, reached the house. Initially his heart sank, there was peeling paint, a drain spout was broken and obviously leaking, and there was a great deal of litter in the gap between the pavement and the basement windows. But it was obviously a house with huge potential. He walked on towards The Ravine, for it was of that the flat had wonderful views. The views were possibly the result of the estate agent's exaggeration. It was a sideways squint to the trees at the top of the ravine, but it was on a quiet road and might be more appropriate.

It was now dusk, and he decided to return to *The Osborne*, without seeing the flat. For the time being he decided to put out of his mind all ideas of moving to Cleadonbridge and resolved not to say anything to Anna about it, at least for the moment. He needed to think. In the meantime he decided to make himself a cup of tea and read the novel he had brought.

He was quite glad that the time had been fixed so late. As he had strolled to St Columba's that morning, he had observed that St. George's was advertising Taizé Worship that evening at 6.30 and he had decided to go. It had been a typical mainstream Anglican church, but now boasted itself as being "inclusive".

He arrived a few minutes before 6.30 and was greeted by a young man, who held out his arms in a welcoming gesture; he spoke quietly, 'It's wonderful to have you with us this evening. I'm Mike.'

'I'm Steven. Do I…'

'Come in!' Mike led the way to the side chapel where a handful of men and women were gathered. 'This is Steven.'

There were quiet murmurs of greeting, and then the service began.

He knew little of the form of worship and the calm, almost soporific chanting was very soothing, but the many repetitions of each chant he found rather boring. Was it supposed to induce some sort of trance? What was it that the leader had said? Was he a priest? He introduced himself simply as James. *Holding oneself in a presence and letting Christ, through the Holy Spirit, pray in us.* Did it "Speak to his condition?" Who used to say that? But no revelation had come, and he had found his mind wandering onto his dinner "date" with Anna and where, if anywhere, it might lead and indeed where he wanted it to lead. He began to wonder if it had been a good idea to come to Cleadonbridge at all.

Coffee and some sort of wine were on offer after the service, but he wanted to get away.

'I'm sorry, I'm meeting somebody,' he apologised. This was of course true, but it was half an hour before he was to meet Anna and the place was just around the corner.

'I hope we may see you again, Steven.' This was from James.

'Oh, I hope so, but…' He fled.

★

The Riviera was easy to locate, and Anna had suggested that they meet there. He had bought a bottle of Barolo at the Tesco Metro he'd spotted on his walk from the bus stop on the first day. Even knowing that the restaurant was a BYO didn't diminish the embarrassment he felt at carrying it in. The interior was dim and was free of the check table cloths and plastic flowers that seemed to be found in most Italian restaurants. Of course this one claimed to be "Mediterranean" rather than Italian.

'Have you a reservation sir?' The waiter, or was it the owner, Konni, spoke in an assured manner and with a slight indefinable accent.

'I believe that Ms. Ashworth made one.'

'Anna?' His face lit up. 'Ah, yes. She said she was entertaining a gentleman.'

Steven could imagine her saying this. He had been struggling to recall who she reminded him of since their first meeting. She was like a well known comedy actress on television, who spoke in a similar coquettish manner.

'Would you come this way sir?' Steven was shown the way to a table for two in the corner. He wondered if this was seen as being a suitable place for a romantic tryst.

Was their meeting that in any sense? His musings were interrupted by Anna.

'Darling! I'm terribly sorry to be late.' She had arrived so unexpectedly that he had not had time to stand to greet her. She kissed the top of his head.

'Ouch!" He grinned. "I know it's bald!'

'It's quite sexy you know! Have you ordered?'

'I've only just arrived and haven't seen the menu yet.'

'Here you are, sir, Anna!'

'Thanks Konni!'

'May I take your coats?' he asked. Anna's was a rather ordinary anorak type of garment, but her dress was now seen, a rather striking black and gold one with sequins. He was glad he retained the jacket and tie he had put on that morning. He preferred some formality when he attended church, but it was mere laziness that he had not changed into more comfortable clothes. He raised his eyebrows and smiled at Anna.

'Do you like it?' She half stood and did a little twirl. 'Oxfam, £2.50. I get a lot of my clothes there; I haven't a large teacher's pension like some!'

'When you are ready, my friends.' Konni had returned with the menu. 'Shall I open that wine for you, sir?'

The menu was much as usual with some interesting variations. He chose *Parsley Tabbouleh* as a starter, wondering if it were possible to make it at home. Anna chose *Dolmades*; he often made that at home as he had leaves from the old vine in the greenhouse. They both decided to try the *Tazgine*, a lamb stew with parsnips, prunes, and chickpeas for the main course and it seemed appropriate to have a rather strong wine. Their conversation flowed as easily as the wine, and they were soon considering whether to have a dessert.

'I really don't think I could manage a dessert.' he said

'Me neither! Let's go back and have coffee and a liqueur or some brandy.' Anna insisted that they shared the bill, and they strolled back, keeping a discreet distance from each other. The distance was maintained as they entered the house on Gilbert Street, Anna leading the way up the stairs to her flat. 'Here, give me your coat!' She disappeared into her bedroom and emerged a few seconds later, having shed her own coat. In the brighter light her dress seemed even more striking, and she seemed to take an almost flirtatious pose as she entered the room.

'How do you like your coffee?' Anna asked.

'Black, bible-black.' He was about to say it was Greg who had first insisted he drank coffee that way but thought it better not to mention his name.

Anna picked up the half quotation. 'Aha, *Under Milk Wood* "Spring, moonless night in the small town, starless and bible-black…" I did that years ago in, Gawd help us, where was it? I was Polly Garter.'

He laughed. 'No better than you should be, missy. We did it in the village. I was the Reverend Eli Jenkins in one part.'

'I seem to remember he names a lot of rivers in one of his poems – that would be good for you as a geographer.'

'And they needed to be pronounced properly. Fortunately, there is an exiled Welshman in the village who came in as language coach.'

'We get professional coaches; they can be a bit of a pain. But I promised you a liqueur. I'll get it while the coffee is gurgling.'

'What have you got?'

'Well there's Drambuie, you know Scotch and honey.'

'I haven't had that for years… yes, let's have that. Reminds me of all the Munroes I haven't done?'

'Monroes? Oh, yes, you told me,' she said rather abruptly. Earlier when they were chatting about the theatre, she had been quite animated.

He sat down on an armchair and sipped his liqueur. On her return from the kitchen with coffee she sat on the settee. For a moment Anna seemed to be about to suggest that he joined her on the settee, but they remained where they were and chatted. Afterwards he could not remember what the subjects had been. Half his mind was trying to work out her intentions.

At about 10.00 she sighed. 'No, Steven.' She spoke quite gently. 'We don't want any more, do we?'

'Any more what?' He affected ignorance, yet he knew what she had been thinking.

'It's been very pleasant talking about old times and our present lives… The theatre and so on. But no more than that?' She raised her eyebrows.

He decided to make light of it. 'Ms Ashworth, I hope you weren't going to suggest that I wanted to have my wicked way with you?'

She hesitated before replying, evidently also deciding to laugh it off. 'As if I would suspect you of being such a villain, Mr. Darlington! And now, I'm going to throw you out. We start rehearsals at 10.00 and I need to get some things done first.'

At the door she offered her cheek, and he kissed it. On the way back to *The Osborne* he reflected that he was glad it had... what was that song? Love ending before it had begun... or something like that. He slept easily. On their first meeting it seemed that Anna was suggesting more; this time he had been prepared to make a move but had been forestalled. They had made no plans; he had another day in Cleadonbridge.

Chapter Six

Monday 28th March 2011

He decided to spend at least another day in Cleadonbridge. There was room in *The Osborne* and, as he told Susan Jamieson when he rang her up, he wanted to explore what he described as "his old haunts".

'You have a lovely holiday, Steven!' She promised to keep an eye on things at *Green Haugh* whilst he was away, and seemed delighted that he wasn't coming back immediately. He knew she would tell everyone in the village and could almost hear her saying, "That nice Mr. Darlington is having a well earned holiday in his old haunts." Like many others, she hinted that he might find someone else; perhaps he might. But he was also considering somewhere else, that he might leave the place where he had lived almost all his life and settle here… he thought of the Yeats poem again. *That is no country for old men.* It was of course, about approaching death and he certainly wasn't yet at death's door. And "no country"? Make it his country! He might help here in some sort of outreach work… perhaps associated with the church.

He didn't attempt to contact Anna. She was, after all, working and she hadn't indicated that she wanted to take things further. Take things further? What did he mean? Was it just stirrings of a sexual desire so long suppressed? Or was he really attracted to her? Was she attracted to him? She had rebuffed his half attempted advance, although on that first meeting she had seemed almost eager, and it had been he who had been reluctant. His staying an extra few days was in part that he might have the opportunity to get to know her better, but he wasn't sure how to suggest they meet for, as far she was aware, he had returned to Devon.

The day was sunny, he could see the hills beyond the town, and on the spur of the moment he decided to go for a walk there. The University Ramblers had regarded these as their especial stamping ground. The Sunday Hike often had the instruction, "Meet 9.30 at Central Station, book day return to Corley Castle." He didn't go every Sunday, for that would mean missing the 11.00 High Mass at St. Columba's, but on the days he did join the ramblers he went to the early Low Mass, forgoing breakfast to do so. He smiled wryly; the congregation at that was about the same size as at the one Mass had attended yesterday. Corley lay on the edge of the Pennines; long tough walks were possible, but he had not thought of bringing his boots and so he would have to take an easier route. He recalled that Meadow Lake Park had some easy paths. Trains, he discovered left just after the hour and the journey took about an hour.

At 11.00 he stepped off the train at Corley; he was the only passenger who got off and the platform was bare. Gone were the attractive chalet style station buildings, the only building was the usual bus shelter on the one platform; the line had been made single track. He made his way down the slope and onto the main road where there was a surprise. Corley had once been a spa; indeed the name of the station had been "Corley Castle and Spa" but there had been no evidence of this function fifty years ago. He understood that there had been a rather feeble flow of a chalybeate spring which was supposed to have almost miraculous curative powers. It attracted a few visitors in Victorian times, but that trade had dried up, as had the spring. The hotel, so described, had been no more than a rather run down pub, which served Cleadonbridge Brewery's rather watery beer. They had seldom patronised it as pubs didn't open until 7.00 on Sunday, which was after their return to the city. It now proclaimed itself *Corley Country House Hotel and Spa*. Of course "spa" today meant a sort of retreat from the world where various treatments such as skin rejuvenation were available; one was "pampered". Mary had never been one for such treatment.

He decided to investigate and to have morning coffee. It seemed as though the spa and hotel were separate from what was still a pub, which was cleaner and better furnished than it had been all those years ago. He went into the bar. Morning coffee came with one of those little cinnamon biscuits that had become so popular; he decided it would be enough for now as he had enjoyed another excellent breakfast before leaving *The Osborne*. 'What on earth am I doing?' he muttered aloud. I've not only without boots, map, compass and all the other things that everyone insisted were necessary on a walk. I've nothing to eat. He could have an early lunch and meander up to Meadow Lake Park. Spotting a map on the wall, he wandered over and tried to memorise the route to Meadow Lake; he observed that it was now officially a country park; presumably this would mean that here were well made paths, suitable for his bootless feet.

He drank the coffee fairly quickly, nibbled the biscuit and then strolled out to make his way to the park. It had been a somewhat neglected area when he had known it, but a great deal of amenity planting had taken place, paths had been constructed and it was obvious that in the season, families would come here. Even today there were a few walkers; he greeted them cheerfully. He reached a clearing in the woods from where the hills beyond could be seen; for the hundredth time he regretted not bringing his boots.

He explored further, finding a path that led out onto the moors. As it was fairly dry under foot, he continued, and within half an hour was on the low summit of the outer rampart of the hills. If I lived in Cleadonbridge, I could come here, and the Lakes. I'm bored with Dartmoor; I've known it and the other moors all my life – this is a more exciting place. There's bound to be a rambling club in the city. He was tempted to go further but without a map and only stout shoes he decided he should return to the hotel at Corley and have some lunch. There were a few people in the bar, just finishing lunch and other tables with cutlery and crockery not yet cleared, showed there had been a fair number in earlier.

'Back again!' He grinned. 'Is it too late for some lunch?' he enquired.

'Not at all, sir.' The barmaid, if such a plump middle aged lady might be so termed, was all smiles. 'There you go!' She handed him a large menu. 'Choose whatever you fancy!'

After a few moments he ordered steak and ale pie and chips with a pint of... for a moment he was bewildered at the range of cask conditioned ales. He chose one of the best known north country brews.

'It will be about ten minutes, sir.' She delivered the order and returned to the bar. 'On holiday are you?'

'Sort of. I was a student at Cleadonbridge about a hundred years ago and I used to come out here with the University Rambling Club.'

She giggled. 'So you are about a hundred and twenty.'

He smiled. 'Actually, it will be fifty years, next year, since I graduated.'

She calculated and then said, 'You don't look your age, if you don't mind me saying it.'

The pie was excellent, as was the beer and he was tempted to order another pint, but he paid his bill and prepared to leave. As he approached the Hotel he had observed that they were a venue for marriages and civil partnerships. If… if he were to get married again… Was he imagining Anna? Of course they would want the ceremony to be in church. But how wonderful it could be; he'd plenty of money, there could be a Nuptial Mass with all the catholic ritual in St. Columba's, or a quiet plighting of their troth in the side chapel. But this is ridiculous, he told himself; it's supposed to be young girls that plan weddings with no especial partner in mind; some in Mary's classes had filled their rough work books with drawings of bridal gowns. But he had someone in mind: Anna. That was only because he had just met her and… Did he love her? Did he only lust after her? Or what was worse, did he just want someone, anyone, for sex? These muddled thoughts took him down to the railway station where he caught the next train.

If he were to sell *Green Haugh* he'd have quite a bit,

enough to buy a nice house, or perhaps a flat like Anna's. His wanderings yesterday had shown that such were available. He could help out in the parish somehow, as he did at home. Money would be needed there too. He began to create a life for himself in Cleadonbridge. Church would be important, but there was also high culture, the art gallery had some wonderful collections and had interesting occasional exhibitions. Then of course there was the theatre, not only *The Kirkgate*, but also *The Princess*, where travelling companies toured, including opera; he could really get into opera. He'd never seen any... grand opera, wasn't it termed? Was Anna interested in such? In one of the churches he'd seen advance publicity for the Passion Plays to be performed in the Cathedral during Holy Week; things like that involved scores of people there might even be a rôle for him there.

★

He decided not to go out to eat that evening. *The Osborne* was prepared to cook a limited number of standard meals; he assumed they would be microwaved. He ordered a lasagne; it was fairly good, and the landlady asked if he would like a salad. She also offered a bottle of wine which was not very good, a sugared red of dubious provenance. But he thanked her profusely and drank some of it, saying he would take the rest to drink later. He took it to his room. As he ate the lasagne, he considered his earlier flights of fancy. Was it so fanciful? Apart from his time at university and the half dozen years in Bristol, he'd lived all his life in or near *Green Haugh*. Was it not time for a change? Life begins at 70! It was quite a pleasant, still evening and he decided to take a stroll through the streets of the area. There were few people about and of course he knew none of them. Had he been at home there might not have been many about, but most of them he would know, at least by sight. Of course, he would get to know people if he lived in Cleadonbridge, but there was certain anonymity about living in a city which appealed. When the boys were born the ladies of the parish gathered round the pram, in later years the ladies observed them as they were on the way to school, and saw, or imagined that they saw, resemblances to his parents; almost every aspect of his life was known to many of the people in the place. The lamps in this city street gave little light, but it was possible to see its Georgian uniformly. He contrasted this with the rather higgledy-piggledy nature of the village. He might create a settled ordered life for himself here… and perhaps be able to share it with Anna. He found himself passing close by her flat. He looked up at the windows of her lounge. The lights were on, but the curtains were drawn. Why had he come here? There was a tiny balcony like feature outside the windows and he almost giggled at the thought of their acting out the scene from *Romeo and Juliet*. Not that they were "star crossed lovers", nor indeed could there be any family feuds to make difficult their becoming… lovers. He dwelt on the word, remaining on the pavement outside the front door, hesitating. He moved towards the door, his hand stretching out for Anna's bell. But he then let it drop. It wasn't appropriate somehow; she thought he had returned to Devon and would be worried at so late a caller, although… he looked at his watch; it was only just turned

8.30. Tomorrow, perhaps… He set off decisively along the street. Beyond The Ravine the lights of the city were spread out below. As he was about to turn the corner, Anna's door opened; he paused, though aware that as there were about half a dozen flats in the building it was not likely to be her. The light from the hallway showed a man, pausing on the steps. He was chuckling. Then came Anna's unmistakeable bell like laughter.

'Oh, Desmond, you are quite the silliest person I know! As if I could after what we've been doing this evening. I've no energy.'

'Well I was game for it, darling! Bye!' He waved his hand and walked down the street towards Steven. The light from the house was cut off as Anna shut the door. Anna's visitor passed close to Steven; he was quite young, no more than forty and very handsome. Fancy Anna having a lover that was twenty years her junior! For a lover he must be. "As if I could after what we've been doing this evening. I've no energy." It must have been sex. Jealousy welled up inside him, although rationally he accepted that this Desmond must have a prior claim. Any hopes he had were now dashed. But what had he hoped for?

Chapter Seven

Tuesday 29th March 2011

The morning after his trip to Corley Steven woke just before 8.00, the time he had set his alarm. He had the impression that the landlady… What was her name? Had she told him? Anyway, he thought that she expected to have all cleared by 9.00.

He had thought that he might try to come to grips with the research issues that he had investigated all those years ago. Denudation chronology had been all the rage in the 1950s and early '60s; he had done a modest dissertation on in as a part of his finals. It was old hat now, but there had been a paper by a young academic, published in an online journal, that had exploded a long held view of erosion surfaces in an area some distance from Cleadonbridge. He had made a copy of this article which he had brought with him, thinking he might be able to study it, if Anna were unavailable. As it was fully referenced, there were a number of leads he might follow. In particular, he wanted to read again the article by Dr. Robinson: Ted Robinson, who was his tutor. The recent paper had been particularly damning of Robinson's work, both his research methods and the conclusions. He knew that the vast resources of the

University Library were available to him, and he hoped not only to read Ted's paper but his PhD on which it was based. What annoyed him about this whippersnapper, as Steven thought of him, was his damming of the methods, when he stated that it was impossible to know how Robinson, who was now dead, had arrived at these conclusions. He had not made the slightest effort to get hold of the thesis. Ted was a gentle and kindly man, somehow middle aged before his time and who had died quite young, from leukaemia, not long after they had graduated. But Steven was sure that Ted was always thorough in his work.

It would give him an excuse to remain longer and perhaps see Anna again. But was there any point in that? She was Desmond's partner it would seem.

'Ah, Mr. Darlington!' The landlady was hovering at the bottom of the stairs.

'Yes, Mrs... You know I'm terribly sorry, I've quite forgotten your name. It must be old age.' He laughed apologetically.

'It's Miss actually, Miss Jones, but do call me Catherine.'

He realised now, there was faint hint of a Welsh accent. 'And I'm Steven.'

'Well Steven, I wondered if you had decided to stay any longer because there's a gentleman e-mailed me this morning and...'

Had Miss Jones – he couldn't think of her as Catherine – asked him last evening immediately after seeing Anna and Desmond, he would have said he wanted to leave now, but the idea of the library investigation appealed. 'I'd like to stay over the weekend if that's OK?'

'That's fine. I'm delighted that you're enjoying the city

again after all these years.' He had told her his reason for visiting Cleadonbridge.

Fortified by the usual excellent "Full English Breakfast" (perhaps it should it be "Full Welsh Breakfast"?) he made his way to the University. To avoid passing Anna's flat he took a slightly circuitous route to the Boulevard where he could catch the bus out to the University. The library was a 1930's mock Georgian block similar to many of the other university buildings.

'Good morning! I was a student here many years ago and wondered if it were possible to register to use the library.'

'Oh, you're an alumni, then?'

Steven winced inwardly at the grammatical solecism but smiled outwardly. 'Yes.'

'You need to fill in this form, get a passport photo; there's a machine in the Union and then bring it back with some sort of ID.'

'Driving licence?'

'That'll be fine. We'll see you later then!'

As he left, he observed that the Latin inscription recalling the first University Librarian now had an English translation next to it. Most of them had not really understood it, but fifty years ago there was an assumption that all educated people knew Latin.

He returned to the Library with a photograph, was duly enrolled and found his way to the book stack where the journal he wanted to consult was shelved. He found the volume and the year and read through the article. It was quite tough going and when he had finished, he decided to have a coffee. The paper had raised more issues and he wanted to explore at least some of them in the thesis; there was also an extensive bibliography.

However, his hopes of reading the thesis were dashed by the librarian. 'I'm afraid that we need twenty four hours notice to produce an academic thesis, Mr. Darlington.' At least that gave him an excuse to remain a little longer in Cleadonbridge.

He spent most of the day on the various learned journals, with only short breaks for lunch and tea. He felt now he was getting somewhere but that he needed to continue the following day or later in the week if the thesis took longer than he expected. On his return to *The Osborne* he again took a roundabout route to avoid passing Anna's flat. What was he afraid of, he questioned himself. If he met her he would be sure to mention seeing her and Desmond the other night and that would be embarrassing. Yet if he didn't, he would be awkward, wanting, and yet not wanting to know what they were to each other. But he had no right to expect anything; he never had.

'Will you want a meal tonight, Mr... err... Steven?' Catherine Jones met him in the entrance hall.

On the spur of the moment he made a decision. 'No thanks Catherine, I thought I'd go into town this evening, perhaps have a drink somewhere and a bite to eat.'

'That's quite all right, just so long as I know. And breakfast tomorrow?'

'8.00? Is that OK?'

'That's fine!' She disappeared into the back of the house. Thankfully, she never seemed to want to chat. One lady like Susan Jamieson was quite enough.

He caught the bus into the city centre and wandered

around for a while. Then he was rather caught unawares in finding himself near *The Kirkgate*. It was the poster that attracted him *Death on the Mersey*. He remembered that Anna had told him about it, a rather silly play she had said. It opened tomorrow and on the spur of the moment he went across the road and found his way to the box office.

'Have you any seats for tomorrow's performance?'

'How many were you wanting sir? We've only got a few odd singles left.'

'That's fine; there's only me!' He chose a seat in the stalls, but which was at the end of a row. He hoped that he would have a good view.

He hurried away, still not wanting to meet Anna, who might or might not be in the theatre at this time and he needed to find a place to eat. What was that pub that Dorothy had found? It was round here somewhere, though he wondered why he should he expect it still to be here, nearly half a century later. She was fascinated by the name; it wasn't *The Pig and Whistle,* she'd first said that, then when they set out to find it, she realised it was… ah, yes, *The Pen and Wig;* it was of course, near the law courts. Hating to appear to be a stranger, he didn't ask but trailed up and down several side streets before he found it. Back then, the best one could hope for would have been a stale pork pie and a bag of crisps, but, as he'd hoped, full meals were served and, as he had also hoped, the place was quiet.

He went in and ordered chicken and mushroom pie and a pint of the local brew. Sitting at a small table in a corner, he expected to remain undisturbed, but was not unduly put out when, as the place filled up, two young men approached and asked if the other chairs at his table were free.

'Of course!' Steven indicated with his hand that they should sit down.

'Thanks mate,' said one of the two.

'Not a bad evening,' Steven suggested.

'Weather or the pub?'

'I meant the weather,' Steven said. 'The pub hasn't changed much since I was last here.'

'When was that?'

'About fifty years ago.'

'In 1961?' one of the two exclaimed.

'Yes. Well, it might have been in 1962, in fact.'

'So, what's that poem…? My Uncle Joe used to say it…

> *'Sexual intercourse began*
> *In nineteen sixty-three*
> *(which was rather late for me) -*
> *Between the end of the "Chatterley" ban*
> *And the Beatles' first LP.*

'I never really understand what it was all about.'

'Luke, you are always going on about sex. I'm beginning to think Melissa isn't giving you enough.'

'Do you know what the Chatterley ban was?' asked Steven.

'Not really.' The young man seemed interested. 'I'm Josh, by the way.'

'And I'm Luke,' his companion added.

'My name's Steven.'

'Great to meet you Steven!' said Luke. Josh nodded his assent.

'Lady Chatterley's Lover is a novel by D. H. Lawrence.

It was banned for obscenity, and then finally published in about 1960 which led to an obscenity trial against Penguin who had published it.'

'What was it about?' asked Josh.

'How was it obscene?' chimed in Luke.

'The story was about the relationship between a Lady Chatterley and a working class man, Mellors, the gamekeeper. It described sex in detail and...' Steven leaned over the table, imparting a mock horror to his tone. 'It used,' he paused dramatically, 'four letter words.'

'Like, well...' Josh paused.

'Fuck?' suggested Luke.

Steven chuckled. 'And others. Almost everyone was fascinated by the trial and copies of the book were circulating. I was a student here at the time and someone took one into a lecture. He even signed the register "Lady Chatterley's Lover" as well as his own name.'

The young men seemed baffled and shook their heads, then Luke asked, 'Hey, you were a student here, what subject did you do?'

'Geography.'

'There's a coincidence. We're doing Geography; final year now.'

'Indeed it is! What are you specialising in?' Steven asked.

Josh answered first. 'I'm getting really into GIS.'

'Ah, Geographical Information Systems. I don't know much about it, but I can see its application in the modern world.'

His friend grinned. 'He thinks he will get a good job with it.'

'It's not just that, I enjoy it...'

'But what about you, Luke?' Steven asked.

'I am concentrating on the geography of minorities; my dissertation was based on that.'

'What is that?'

'It's a range of topics including social exclusion... such as trying to find a cohesion policy that deals with socio-geographic inequality. In my dissertation I...'

'Hey, we're on a break, Luke. Give it a rest.'

'It does sound more like sociology, I must say, but,' Steven said, rising, 'I want another pint. Can I get you both another?'

'That's very kind of you. We're both on the Cleadon Wolf.'

They chatted for about half an hour then, partly because he wanted to go back to *The Osborne* and partly because he felt it was unfair to intrude on them further, he excused himself. As it was a clear still night he walked back. There was always a belief that times had changed and changed for the worse, but Steven was an optimist and believed that change was often for the better. One that had come out that evening was the greater equality. Had he and some of his fellow students met a seventy year old man, the latter would have expected, and in general would have been granted, a due deference. At home it was still a bit "the rich man in his castle, the poor man at his gate". There was still a deference to, well, not the squirearchy; such hardly existed in his part of Devon, but to those who lived in the larger houses in the upper part of the town who might be considered in such terms. The city was more egalitarian and that appealed to him. He also had enjoyed the buzz in the city and tomorrow he would be going to see Anna in a play at *The Kirkgate*. It was with this pleasant thought that he reached "home". How would it be if home was really in this area?

Chapter Eight

Wednesday 30th March 2011

The next day he had become so involved in establishing the methods and conclusions of yesteryear's geomorphologists and in reading the PhD thesis to find out precisely what methods Ted Robinson had used, that he almost lost track of time. He was disappointed to realise that dear Dr. Robinson was not slapdash, as the young academic had implied, but rather imprecise, although arguably it was impossible to be precise about the conditions in the geological past. He had stopped for lunch, but realised it was now teatime; he debated whether to eat before or after the theatre. He also wondered whether he might try to meet Anna and if so, before, or after the play.

In the event the decision was taken out of his hands. He decided to go into the city centre to find somewhere to eat before the play and was passing the theatre at 6.00. Anna was just crossing the street. They recognised each other simultaneously.

'Steven darling!'

'Anna, d...' He was about to repeat the endearment but thought better of it and smiled and waved. They met beside an alley leading to what he assumed was the stage door.

'I thought that you had long since departed for Glorious Devon!'

'Well, I couldn't tear myself away from this beautiful city.'

'Oh, and I thought it must be that you wanted to see me!' She hung her head in mock misery, looking up at him with a pleading and mockingly seductive expression; at least he assumed it was mockery. He was embarrassed, for it was, in part, what he had stayed on for.

'Well... I wanted to revisit some of the places I used to go to and there was something I wanted to look up in the University Library. I don't suppose I'll be coming back...' He spoke in a rush.

'Look, darling, I can't stop, but we must meet before you go. What are your plans for tonight?'

'I'm coming to tonight's performance and...'

'The opening night? I hope we are up to scratch. Meet me in the foyer after the final curtain.'

As he wandered away, he thought that Anna seemed genuinely pleased to see him and that perhaps they might be able to explore various possibilities... if Desmond were no more than a passing fancy. He considered various possibilities for dinner but settled on a pizza in a small restaurant which promised "the real Italian taste".

★

Steven realised that the play was a spoof of *Death on the Nile* and was pleased that it was based on the 1978 film that he and Mary had seen not long after Paul was born. The original play, which they had once read with the thought of presenting it in the village, was quite different.

This play was restricted in its scope compared with the film. It was set in the late 1960s on board *The Royal Buttercup*, an exclusive private hire cruiser on the Mersey with a call at New Brighton where the party went to a dance in the Tower Ballroom. The shipboard scenes were on a restricted stage, which when the curtain closed briefly, had miraculously become a lavish ballroom. He marvelled at this; such was quite beyond the resources of the dramatic society at home; the parish hall was very limited, although they did their best. He thought of the appreciative gasp of the audience when the curtain went up in revealing the bare boards and wall transformed into something such as a middle class lounge; it was something that always amused both of them. Mary had usually been involved in the set design.

The twists and turns of the plot of this play were not always clear, but some of the characters bore recognisable similarity to those in the film. Adrian Hatchman, the pompous solicitor who took charge was a little bit like Poirot. Anna's was a good part, but quite short because she was shot about halfway through the play. As a gossip columnist on *The Liverpool Express* she had written something possibly quite true about a Mrs. Bankes-Browne, but which had been seen as libellous. Steven marvelled at the subtle way the two spoke with 'Scouse" accents, somehow achieving the appropriate class level. Bankes-Browne was "posh" but her accent came through in her soupy tones. It was only later that he realised that the name of Anna's character, Sandra Otterspool was not only close to the name in the film, Salome Otterbourne, but it was an area of Liverpool where Mary had lived in her final years as a student in the city. The two women who were associated with the young man, Dizzy Dave, were not at all like Jacqueline de Bellefort and Linnet Ridgeway, except perhaps in their names, Jacky and Loopy Lou; the latter had managed to obtain much of the money from their covert drug dealing and it transpired that they had been supplied by Dave with drugs. It was not clear if Sandra's accusations were about this or something else. Bankes-Brown was prominent in local politics… of course everyone or almost everyone had a reason to hate someone he thought and to harbour murderous thoughts if not actually commit murder.

The best part was a scene in the ballroom where Sandra almost seized Patrick Breen, the friend and golfing companion of Adrian and danced, not a tango as Angela Lansbury and David Niven had done, but to the tune *Yellow Submarine*, did a slinky parody of dance. Steven was, for those few moments, quite riveted; this was Anna's home. She was thoroughly enjoying the part. Steven drifted into a reverie; he recalled how, not long before Mary's illness had begun, *Death on the Nile* had been shown on television. They had tried to imitate the antics of the two on screen, but Mary collapsed, saying, amid giggles that they hadn't space in the sitting room and in any case, she wanted to watch the film. He had looked at her; she was clutching her side and breathing heavily. She insisted it was nothing, but it was the first inkling they had of her illness. He sighed deeply and turned his attention to the stage.

After the performance Anna arrived surprisingly

promptly, bright and – he hesitated to think – bouncy, but she was certainly cheerful. 'Now I'm not going to ask you what you thought of our little offering; I somehow think it's not quite your thing.'

He was embarrassed again. 'Well, it's not quite that, but I never really sorted out quite what was what. It seemed immensely complicated.'

'No, we found it very confusing at first reading.' She laughed. 'And at second reading too. But it was such great fun. We actually got a guy from the local dance school to work out the choreography for the *Yellow Submarine* scene. That was damned hard work.'

'It looked sort of spontaneous and, well, not clumsy but...' He was at a loss to find words.

'That's what's so clever about it. It's like having to do bad acting.'

'What do you mean?'

'When you have a character who is supposed to be acting a part and doing it badly.'

'We have enough of the ones who are just bad actors.' He chuckled at a recollection. 'On one dreadful occasion in the pantomime, dear Mrs. Lewis dried up and stood there, then came out with, "Oh dear. I knew it last night". Fortunately, it passed, as the whole show was chaotic, more or less intentionally so.'

'That can happen even with the professional theatre. We are not always perfect. It's one of the many delights of the job. There was a review once of a West End play which stated, "The prompt, although unseen, quickly became a firm favourite with the audience.".'

'No! Were you...?'

'Not me, nor anyone I knew, but it does happen.' A familiar figure passed them. 'Bye, Desmond!' she called.

Anna's visitor of the other night. He tried to speak casually. 'Is he one of the company? Oh yes, of course, he had the role of the Socialist, Eòin MacFhearghuis, who had denounced everyone including the audience, as bloodsuckers and waved *Socialist Worker* around.' Had he scored one on the young man? Seeing him in the full light of the foyer he realised that he was perhaps even younger than he had first thought; and he was indeed many years Anna's junior. Were they lovers? There seemed now to be almost a coolness between them, but perhaps he had stolen a march on Desmond. Or perhaps they had had a row.

She laughed. 'Yes, it's his first big role and he's done really well. Scowling in the corner and mouthing all the left wing slogans. Anyway, are we going to go for a drink?'

'Aren't you all going out on the razzle? I thought that you and Desmond and, all the others…'

'No – we can't do that every time. We have a month's run!'

'So, what shall we do? A drink in a pub or a coffee?'

'We could have a drink at my place; I have still some things left from Christmas.'

'That would be nice. I know…' He made an effort to overcome his embarrassment about the whole situation. 'Why don't we get a taxi? I've got…'

'Loadsamoney!' Anna spoke in a cockney accent.

Steven was surprised. 'Err…?'

'You know, the character invented by Harry Enfield in the 1980s. His catchphrase was "loadsamoney!".' Seeing his bewilderment she laughed. 'No, I don't suppose that's your thing either, darling.' She kissed his cheek. 'But it's a lovely evening, let's walk.' She slipped her hand into his and they set off along the street away from the city centre, with its shops and offices and the theatre and up the hill to the Georgian Quarter.

'Do you remember what Doctor Johnson said about London?' Steven said.

'When a man is tired of London, he is tired of life?' she replied.

'He went on to add, "...for there is in London all that life can afford." Is that not true of Cleadonbridge?'

'How do you mean?'

'Here,' he said, gesturing to the area they were leaving, 'are all the shops one might want, theatres, art galleries, museums...'

'Only one of each of those last two.'

He made a dismissive gesture. 'And then where we're going is an area of gracious living, now revived and a wonderful place to live.'

'It can be a bit fraught at times, but yes, it's a good place to live,' she agreed.

'And everything is more democratic in the city.'

'Democratic?'

'Well, egalitarian.' He described his meeting with Josh and Luke. 'At home it is still rather, "The rich man in his castle, The poor man at his gate, God made them high and lowly..." and a sort of settled, unchanging order and...'

'So here it is dynamic, thrusting?'

'I sometimes wish that I had stayed in Bristol, enjoying city life. Living in the country has many advantages, but...' his voice tailed off.

'Well, you could live in Cleadonbridge or anywhere else for that matter, now that you are footloose and fancy free.'

'I'm seriously considering it.'

'Are you?' She spoke almost archly.

'But I don't want to rush into anything.'

'Of course not. By the way, are you hungry? I could really enjoy some fish and chips and the place on the corner is very good. Look!' She pointed.

He grinned. 'I did have a pizza before the play, but why not!' It seemed almost decadent.

They bought two fish and one portion of chips and hurried along the street.

'Here we are.' She inserted her key into the lock and motioned him to go in.

She led the way to the kitchen, set the parcel on the table, opened a cupboard, and pulled out two dinner plates, then rummaged in a drawer and produced cutlery. 'I thought that we'd be civilised; Mummy would expect no less.' She giggled.

He was amused to observe that the plates were of a superior design and that the cutlery was the "correct" type. 'Real fish knives and forks!' he commented.

'Fish eaters,' she corrected him. 'Isn't that what Miss Mitford told us?'

'I'm not sure; I thought Betjeman started that one. "Phone for the fish knives, Norman…" Fish knives and forks were arriviste, those with old money would have inherited cutlery, along with everything else, and would not have them.'

'Really? I know Mummy always insisted on our saying "fish eaters".'

He marvelled silently at the deference that she paid to her long dead parents, or at least her mother. He shrugged. 'What does it matter? Anyway, neither Nancy Mitford nor John Betjeman would have eaten chip shop food.'

'Oh I could imagine Sir John might. He might even have written a poem about it.' She had divided the food onto the two plates and indicated that he should sit down. 'Would you like a lager? I've got a couple of bottles in the fridge.'

'Mmm, please!'

They tucked into the meal; surprisingly he found he was quite hungry.

'This is good, nice crisp batter and not swimming in grease like those in the village chip shop at home.'

'Do you patronise it?'

'I wouldn't do so often, even if it was any good, but I hardly ever use it because it is very second rate. It's just sometime easier now that I'm on my own. I can and do cook; I did when Mary was alive, and the boys were at home. I enjoy it but sometimes it doesn't seem worth it. This place might be one of the reasons for coming to live in Cleadonbridge.' He laughed.

She laid her cutlery down and looked directly at him. 'And what would the other reasons be…?' She paused, and then placed her hand on his. 'Steven?'

He longed to say what he really felt, that he wanted to settle down with her, but he wasn't sure if indeed that was the case. He wanted to explore the possibility, to get to know her. He also was never sure when she was serious. He laughed nervously. 'Well there's the culture, like theatre. You and *The Kirkgate* are really good and the big places that get the operas and so on and it isn't as if one can't get out into the countryside and these days one can get easily to London and…'

Her hand remained on his. She smiled, squeezed his hand, and then resumed eating. 'Has anyone ever produced a Good Fish and Chips Guide, I wonder?'

'I'm sure someone should.' He felt more relaxed and smiled.

'Like the church guide?' she suggested.

'Of course, that one that told you where the good catholic things were to be found – reserved sacrament, vestments, confessions, daily Mass and so on.' It was easier talking about things like that, things now past. 'Old… what was his name…? Jackson, Forbes Jackson, never went anywhere without it, whatever it was called. It told him where he would find a "good" church.'

'Did you seek out "good" churches on your trips?' she asked.

He smiled. 'Sometimes. And Forbes wouldn't go without what was it called? The manual that told you how to serve at the altar and how many candles on the altar for which sort of service and which should be lit first and so on. Fortescue, that was it, *The Ceremonies of the Roman Rite Described*.'

'I know it was important to some, including Mummy.'

'One thing I remember,' he said, 'you had a dish and cruets on a towel.'

'Cruets?'

'The little bottles with water and wine. The wine cruet had to be in the right hand. Or was it the left? The

123

water cruet was in the other, and you had to wait until the celebrant comes, bow and hand the cruets to the priest swopping them over somehow.'

'Did you always remember which hand for which cruet when you and Forbes and all the others were up at the altar?'

'Most of us didn't worry too much about such niceties. Forbes did, though I can't recall that one in particular.'

'I wouldn't know. Being a girl, I wasn't privileged to serve at Mass. Let me see…' She picked up the pepper and salt. 'These will do. This can be water and this… oh, heavens, I should have provided you with vinegar for your chips; that would be more like wine too.'

'I never bother with it. I like food *au naturel*. But…' He giggled. 'All this talk of cruets; it might be easier to do a guide to fish and chips. Which hand should the salt pot be held in as the sales assistant dredges your chips? That could be a telling point in distinguishing good and bad places, though really the quality of the food is the key.'

'Perhaps we might do that together darling.' Her tone was dismissive, and he remembered that the endearment was meaningless in theatrical circles. In any case, what about Desmond, he thought.

As if she had read his thoughts, she mentioned her fellow actor. 'Desmond is into that sort of thing.'

'Fish and chips?'

'No, all the old Anglo Catholic stuff. He goes to St. Cuthbert's.'

'Ah!' He wasn't prepared to condemn a man he didn't know. He'd said his piece about St Cuthbert's. A silence fell over the table.

Anna broke it, pushing away the plate she announced, 'I've had enough. They are quite good but a bit too greasy for me to eat any more.'

Steven smiled ruefully 'I'm afraid I am inclined to agree. As my late mother would have said, my eyes were greedier than my tummy.'

'You go through into the sitting room. I'll make some coffee. You do want some?'

'Of course!'

What happened next, he was never able fully to remember. Coffee was brought, she motioned him to join her on the settee, they moved closer.

'Now then,' he joked, 'what would Desmond say?'

'Whatever do you mean?'

'Well, aren't you and he…?' His voice trailed away.

'Whatever gave you that idea?' She seemed almost angry.

'I saw him leaving your flat on Monday evening and your final words to him were, "…as if I could after what we've been doing this evening. I've no energy".'

Anna's pealing laughter quite disconcerted him. 'My dearest Steven, we'd had a fiendish rehearsal lasting quite late, Desmond is a fitness fanatic and had persuaded me to go to his gym, and we came back here for a coffee. Then he suggested a walk in the Park. No sex, I promise you. You have put two and two together and made twenty two.'

Steven wasn't sure if he was relieved or sorry. He had drawn away from her when she seemed angry at his comment about her visitor. She now pulled him to her and within seconds it seemed they were struggling to be free of their clothes in a desperately urgent search for fulfilment, for penetration. They ended up panting, on the floor. He had forgotten the intense physical sensations associated with sex. He lost himself in achieving orgasm and was soon pulling away, sated, and also feeling guilty. He had never had sex with anyone other than Mary. He wanted to leave now and never see Anna again.

'That was wonderful, darling. The pleasures of the flesh never pall, do they?' She nuzzled his ear as she spoke. 'But next time you might remember that I am Anna, not Mary. She was your wife, wasn't she?'

'Yes. Oh hell, I'm sorry. I never…' He hardly liked to acknowledge his lack of experience; he guessed she had had many partners. But she spoke of "next time". She might now want to settle down and… His musings were interrupted.

'And perhaps you might not be in quite so much of a hurry!' She kissed him and then stood up. 'Heavens, is that the time? I shall be exhausted tomorrow if I don't get some sleep. No post coital cigarette or whatever the non smokers' equivalent is. I'm going to throw you out!' She spoke firmly.

'When can we meet again?'

'Oh, panting for more sex already?' She patted his face playfully.

He was embarrassed. 'No, it's just that…' He stopped, unsure of what to say, for his mind was running on, imagining planning their future together.

'I'm not going to suggest tomorrow, because I shall want to get a good night's rest and Friday is a bit problematic.' She didn't enlarge on the problem, and he didn't feel it right to ask. 'But Saturday night? Someone is bound to have a party after the play; you could come along, then we might,' she said, playfully tapping his nose, 'let's see.'

As he made his way back to the B&B he was, he felt, almost dancing on air. This could become his home, living in that flat and paying his full share of course, or perhaps buying a smaller house and restoring it, in the dreadful phrase, "to its former glory", its Georgian splendour. With these happy thoughts he slept easily.

Chapter Nine

Thursday 31ˢᵗ March 2011

The next day, Thursday, he woke with an idea, or rather two ideas, which he clarified over breakfast. The first was to finish his studies, and the second was arrange a day on the hills on Friday. There were a few odds and ends he wanted to tie up on denudation chronology, so he would spend the morning in the Library. Then he would investigate the possibility of getting to the Lake District and doing some real walking, for which he would need boots. He could buy a pair of new lightweight ones so that he would be able to get onto the fells; the forecast indicated fine, mild weather. He decided that hiring a car was the best option for getting there. He planned the day almost like a military operation, arriving at the Library just after 9.00. Finishing earlier than he had anticipated, he went into the city centre, where on the outskirts, he found a car hire firm and arranged to pick up a Fiesta the next day.

He had known the place so long ago and had not yet explored it fully; he knew it would have changed. He wandered down Cathedral Street.

'That was it!' he said aloud.

'What was that then?' He turned and saw that he was

being addressed by an older lady; she was wearing clothes that were comfortable, rather than smart. She spoke rather nervously in cultured middle class tones and smiled in a rather nervous way.

She thinks I'm batty of course; I am probably older than she is, and I could be losing it. 'I think that,' he said, pointing to an elaborate shop front, 'was a real grocers' shop, years ago now.'

'That's right!' She seemed relieved that he was not an escaped patient from a mental institution. 'Graham and Gray. My mother would never buy her groceries from anywhere else.'

'I remember it from when I was a student here, nearly half a century ago.' He laughed apologetically. 'We couldn't afford to shop there!'

'No, whatever else it was, it was not cheap.'

'Actually we did treat ourselves to some of the special coffees. Most of the guys in hall used instant but someone's mum had bought him a coffee filter jug and we used to make real coffee. There was a special blend, I think.'

'Yes, G and G. I think it was from Kenya.'

'But did they have the range of cheeses that even a modest supermarket stocks nowadays?'

'I don't believe they did. But we were not used to funny foreign food.' She laughed. 'Actually, there is a stall in the Market Hall that has a superb range. It's called *The Cheese Shack*.'

'I might check it out. I'm only here on holiday and then heading back home to Devon, I could take some with me, but please excuse me, I need to get on.'

'Nice to have met you.'

Most of the buildings along the street were as he remembered, though uses had changed. Fifty years ago, the buildings appeared almost to have been made of the coal on which the city's original prosperity was based. Now they were revealed in a variety of colours; most were the pale yellow local sandstone, but others were in granite and Portland stone. One, which seemed to shriek at the others, was in red brick Edwardian Gothic. Both the architectural style and the building material seemed at variance with the nature of the street yet it had a dignity of its own. Seeing W.H. Smith, he went in and, making the spur of the moment decision to go to the north east of the District, he bought the relevant Ordnance Survey map and a pocket guide to walks, intending to study them over lunch and make plans.

Was it deliberate he thought afterwards? Once settled in the pub he had chosen, he spread out the map and was immediately drawn to the eastern shore of Ullswater. There it was, *The Sharrow Bay*, where he and Mary had spent their honeymoon. If he parked there or perhaps a bit further on at Howtown, he could make the ascent of Place Fell, as he and Mary had done. He wondered if the tiny church in Martindale was still open; they had gone to Morning Service there on the Sunday, almost by accident, passing it as they made their way to Place Fell. They had returned by steamer along the lake, but he did not think that they would be running at this time of the year. Place Fell was not too high and he was still fit enough to get up that. Lunch – would Catherine make him some sandwiches and a flask? She probably wouldn't have the latter; he could buy one at the climbing shop, but she would, no doubt, fill it for him. He checked the little guide book on Place Fell. "…at 657 metres it is not one of the highest peaks, but it has glorious view."

'Here you are, sir, sausage and chips and a pint of best bitter!' His thoughts were interrupted by the arrival of his meal; he put the map away lest it get splashed before he had even used it on the hills. But he returned to the area in his imagination. Would Anna love the hills as he did, as Mary had done? He feared she would not, but perhaps she would come to enjoy them as he did.

After lunch he wandered into the new, rather soulless shopping precinct that had been built a little after he was a student. It had involved the demolition of a number of the yards with their delightful mixture of former cottages and stables and workshops. He hated this sort of town planning, but he knew he would find what he wanted. There was a "Mall Guide". 'Why,' he muttered to himself, 'do we have to use the American term.' But it did enable him to find one of a well known chain of climbing and outdoor shops.

'Good afternoon, I am looking for a pair of lightweight boots.'

'Sure, mate.' The young man led him to a display of various types of outdoor footwear. 'These are pretty good, not 100% waterproof though…' He handed the boots to Steven. 'Special offer at the mo, £34.99.'

Mate, indeed, he thought. No due deference to his age and the fact of his being a customer, but that was surely better than the obsequious subservience he knew people of his parents' generation expected. In any case, Steven had the other evening been saluting the more egalitarian nature of Cleadonbridge. Aloud he said, 'They'd be good enough

in summer in dry areas, which is where I want them for.'
He did not add that they were cheaper than the sort he
usually wore, which cost nearly £100. 'But...'

'Where are you going to use them?'

'The Lake District!' Steven laughed apologetically.
'Tomorrow,' he added.

'The forecast is good, better than today; it was pissing
down when I came into work. But I wouldn't recommend
them for the Lakes, mate.'

Nevertheless, he went ahead with the purchase, and
he added a waterproof jacket at £59.99, more than he
really wanted to pay. At the last moment he remembered
a vacuum flask, which cost £9.99. Over £100 just to
enable him to take a trip to the Lakes and he had all this
at home. At least he had brought all his clothing and so
on in a rucksack, so he didn't need to buy another. But
he recalled that he kept reminding himself that he had
plenty of money; he remembered Anna's, laughing about
"Loadsamoney".

His sons and many others he knew, even some of
his contemporaries, had "smart phones" that could be
used to access the internet, and he wished he owned
one. However, if he went to the public library, which
was just around the corner, he could use one of their
computers. He soon gained access to a computer and
within a few minutes found out that the journey time by
car from Cleadonbridge to Howtown would be less than
two hours and somewhat to his surprise discovered that
there were steamers from Howtown for Glenridding at
10.20 and 12.35. The former would be a better bet. It was
about 11 km. over Place Fell from Glenridding and would

take three to four hours, which as the steamer arrived at 10:55 would mean that he'd be back in time for tea. Tea at Howtown or perhaps go on to Sharrow Bay and have a splendid afternoon tea there. He should have enough time, at a pinch, even if he were to catch the later boat. It was now 3.30. He pulled out his notebook where he had written down the planned timetable for today, observing that he had finished at about the time he had intended to do. He had no further things planned, he didn't want to try to contact Anna so decided to stay in *The Osborne* for a meal. Remembering the rather awful wine she provided last time, he stopped off at the Tesco Metro and bought a light red wine from the Loire.

On his return to, he asked Catherine Jones about a meal.

'Well, Steven,' she said, 'I've got the lasagne you had the other evening and roast chicken dinner for one.'

'That last one sounds good.'

'And would you like a bottle of wine again?' she asked.

'I wasn't sure that you would have any more, so I bought a bottle earlier.' He produced it from his bag. 'I'm sorry.'

'That's all right. What time do you want dinner?'

He looked at his watch. 'Well, it's only four thirty, so not for a little while.'

'How about 6.00?'

'Fine… until 6.00 then.' He turned and went up the stairs to his room. Once there he kicked off his shoes and lay on the bed contemplating the events of the day. It should be a great day tomorrow and a preliminary to a new life. He studied the guide book again, although he had memorised it already, then relaxed and opened the novel he had brought with him.

The chicken dinner was a bit like school meals, but acceptable. Even so he did not linger over it. He needed to have an early night, but it was far too early to settle down; the novel bored him, so he set off for a walk. Then he had an unsettling thought. About thirty years ago there had been riots in inner Liverpool, an area not unlike this. Indeed, he wondered if it was safe to be walking about here, on his own at night. As he turned towards the Boulevard, his fears surfaced. A small knot of black lads, late teens, he would judge, were standing on the corner, laughing and pushing at each other in a mock fight.

'Ah go on, ya begger.'

'Fuck off, you!'

'Fuck off, yaself!'

Steven didn't avoid them, but as he passed then called out cheerily, 'Night, lads!'

'Have a good night, mate!' called one; the others chorused similarly.

There we are, he thought, there is no need to worry. He realised that he had not explored the area where the Thomas and Ashworth families had lived. It was quite a trek; afterwards he reckoned it must have been nearly three kilometres. The street lighting was not as bright in Park Crescent, and he could only just make out the two houses, but they seemed to be no longer in domestic use, which was a pity, as a flat in one of those would be delightful.

Another line from *Sailing to Byzantium* came to him.

And therefore I have sailed the seas and come
To the holy city of Byzantium.

It was ridiculous to think of Cleadonbridge as a holy city; yet if he lived here, it might be a new beginning, a rebirth. With these confused thoughts he made his way back to *The Osbourne*, and a good night's sleep.

Chapter Ten

Friday 1st April 2011

It was rather later than he had intended before he left *The Osborne*. He picked up the Fiesta at 8.15 and steered his way out through the traffic on the road towards Penrith. He realised that he would miss the 10.20 steamer from Howtown and indeed, frustratingly, as he arrived, he saw her heading out of the bay on the voyage up the lake. Moreover, he found that there was no car parking near the steamer pier. He considered turning the car round and driving back to the *Sharrow Bay*. It had been an incredible extravagance to stay there for the honeymoon and they hadn't really been able to afford it, but now... his mind raced on, imagining himself and Anna staying there... He had read somewhere, "The Sharrow Full Afternoon Tea is unrivalled in the Lake District," but he thought it better not to try, either now for morning coffee or later for afternoon tea itself, only then discovering that they would not be prepared to admit a rambler with rucksack and muddy boots.

The next sailing was 12.35. Then he remembered the little church at the top of the Hause; he tried to recall its dedication. It was only a short distance, and he could park there. This would actually be more convenient when he had finished the walk over Place Fell. He wondered if it would still be functioning as a church and whether it would be open. The one at the top of the hill was the nineteenth century "new" church. The medieval church was further up the dale and not on his route. He reached it in a few minutes, remembering as he arrived that it was St. Peter's. He was relieved that there was a car park, beside the simple gothic structure, what the Victorians thought a church should be. The notice board showed that there was a service every other Sunday. The door was unlocked, and he was delighted to enter that unmistakeably Anglican ambience. He picked up a Book of Common Prayer that was at the back of the church. That was still in use then and he found the order for Morning Prayer; he could imagine he and Mary were here together… Here it was, the old, once familiar words they must have said:

Almighty and most merciful Father; We have erred, and strayed from thy ways like lost sheep. We have followed too much the devices and desires of our own hearts. We have offended against thy holy laws. We have left undone those things which we ought to have done; And we have done those things which we ought not to have done; And there is no health in us.

But there was no time to dwell on the past, perhaps he and Anna… surely she too would love this place. He knew he could get a coffee on the boat and save his lunch until he had at least made some progress on the planned walk. He walked briskly back to Howtown.

The voyage up the lake in the little nineteenth century steamer was glorious, the spring sunshine bringing out the variation between the dark green of the conifers, the bare leafless deciduous trees and the bronze of the bracken. He remembered how on the part of the walk over Sleet Fell he and Mary had struggled with waist high bracken; there wouldn't be the same problem today with last year's fronds battered and lying on the ground.

'Now then, young man, what are you looking so wistful for?' The speaker was an older man, sitting opposite him on the top deck. He was clad in walking gear and, Steven noted, wearing good boots.

Steven smiled. 'I'm just thinking of past triumphs… I've climbed most of the peaks you can see.' He swung his arm round embracing the Helvellyn range, the tops around Kirkstone and of course his objective today, Place Fell.

'I suppose you started young?'

'Well yes. I was a student at Cleadonbridge in the '60s and the university rambling club had weekends here.'

'Lucky you! I never walked the fells until I met Nancy.' He indicated a woman of a similar age who was sitting next to him. She was also dressed for fell walking.

'We married quite late,' she said. 'Well, we'd both been married before but had lost our partners. I used to ramble over the fells with Jim, my first husband. We were in the Melcester Rambling Club.'

'My idea of a good holiday,' put in her husband, 'was to go somewhere warm and lie in the sun.'

'And, Jack,' put in his wife, 'get a little tipsy.'

'Well now I have a pint in the pub when we've done a

walk, not that it's like those that you and Jim did; I'm too old and creaky.'

'Eh. Jack, I can't manage the high tops now either. I'm just grateful that I can do a bit, even get to the top of one or two low fells. And I am thankful to have someone to do it with.' She patted her husband's arm affectionately.

'What are you going to do today?' asked Jack.

'Place Fell. I've just about got time to do it.'

'That's a bit much for us now,' put in Nancy. 'We walked from Glenridding this morning along the lake shore to Howtown.'

'So,' asked Jack, bending towards his wife and kissing her cheek, 'have I earned my pint when we get to Patterdale?'

She returned his kiss. 'We'll see… if you're a good boy.' He hung his head in mock humility.

Their conversation proceeded along similar lines until the end of the short voyage. He walked with them for the mile or so to Patterdale and said his good-byes, thanking Jack for his offer to treat him to a pint, but pleading the need to get on his way. But the conversation had given him hope, even inspiration. If Jack had been converted by Nancy, surely he could persuade Anna to enjoy the fells. Who could not be entranced by their beauty? And Jack was older than Anna.

By 1.30 he was crossing the fields to the foot of Place Fell, following the route suggested in the guide book. Sunset was about seven thirty. Had he time to complete the walk in daylight? He decided to risk it, but found the ascent of 500 metres in two kilometres quite stiff; it took him until nearly until 4.00 to reach the summit trig point. The view was indeed glorious, as the guide book had suggested. He then realised that he hadn't eaten the sandwiches he had brought; it wasn't a day when he had become dehydrated, so he hadn't needed the flask of coffee. He sat down to admire the view and have this belated lunch. Below to the east were Boredale and Bannerdale, then the Kentmere Fells and High Street. To the west he could see most of the three reaches of Ullswater, beyond the lake Helvellyn and Fairfield stood up boldly. Another day and he could venture up there. If he and Anna came to this area, he might introduce her to fell walking. Begin with something small… actually it would be better to go to Keswick than *Sharrow Bay*; he had spent the honeymoon with Mary here and it would be too full of memories. A new start demanded a new place, Keswick with its *Theatre By The Lake* would surely appeal to Anna and Cat Bells would be a wonderful first mountain. They'd taken the boys there; it still meant something to them judging by his conversation with Paul the other day.

'Is that a late lunch or an early tea?' The speaker was a man of about 60 who had approached quietly; Steven had not seen him coming.

'It's a very late lunch, I sort of got delayed and it's taken me longer to get up here than I thought.'

'Which route?'

'Up from Patterdale to Boredale Hause, then up from there.'

His fellow walker grunted. 'I've come up the other way.' He gestured. 'A route I haven't done before although I've done all the Wainwrights.'

'The Wainwrights? Oh, of course.' Steven recalled the pictorial guides to the fells produced by Alfred Wainwright, or "AW", as he now always seemed to be named. 'How many are there?'

'Two hundred and fourteen.' He spoke with some pride. 'I'm well on the way to completing them for the second time. This, at 657 metres is number 108 in order, although…' He laughed. 'AW would have said 2,154 feet. How many have you done?'

'I don't know. I live in the South West so don't get much opportunity.'

'Always a problem. Like AW I got a job here so that I can spend all my spare time on the fells.'

'What's your job?'

'Solicitor, just a small high street firm in Keswick. I am a partner. No real pressure.'

'I was a teacher. My wife and I did cone here several times and…'

'Teachers' holidays – one good summer and you could have bagged them all. But it's better on your own, just leave your wife to get on with shopping and things that women do. Get out onto the fells! Anyway, I'm off! Good rambling!' He shouldered his rucksack and was off, soon disappearing along the ridge towards Boredale Hause.

That's not what I want, Steven thought, but time was pressing and so he made his more cautious descent, not continuing over to Sleet Fell but dropping down into Boredale. The final pull up to The Hause he found wearying and it was dropping dark before he retrieved the car, and had to drive without a pause to ensure he returned it by 9.00.

Chapter Eleven

Saturday 2nd April 2011

Steven surfaced late and had a leisurely breakfast. It all seemed so perfect. He and Anna were so obviously right for each other, with their shared love of the theatre, and other aspects of high culture. She had the flat near St. Columba's; if he sold *Green Haugh* they could have a country cottage in the Lakes somewhere and go there at weekends, have mad parties with the theatre people. It would be like being young again; he felt that the theatre was free of the ageism so prevalent elsewhere; in fact, he reflected, that was also the case in the drama group at home. He was not going to see Anna until after the play when they were to go to a party, and he spent the day in a sort of dream, planning all sorts of thing about how their life together might be. Sometime he would "pop the question". He could do some further academic research; he could register for a Master's degree. It would not be expensive, and he would have plenty of time to work on… on what? Denudation chronology was no longer an area that was investigated, partly of course because it was difficult to be precise about the data. But there would be some aspect of geomorphology he might be able to work on. Another day in the library might give him some ideas.

In the morning as it was raining; he went to the City Art Gallery, which had a fine collection of nineteenth century watercolours. He had decided to leave any academic study for another day and explore some of the city's culture. Normally he found such art rather insipid; today he thought them entrancing. He had a sandwich and a bowl of soup in the art gallery's café. By 2.00 the rain had stopped and the sun had come out.

He decided to go for a walk in The Ravine. As on Sunday in the park, he looked for signs of spring, new life returning. Perhaps that is symbolic, he thought. Perhaps that is just what I am doing, a new life, a life with Anna. Daffodils were thrusting up in the sheltered area; by the gate there were crocuses in abundance, the patterns of purple, blue and yellow seeming, when he narrowed his eyes, almost like an abstract painting. He wondered where he might create a similar feature in his own garden, and then recalled that he was intending to leave Devon. He was impatient to push on with his plans and was finding himself bored and yet at the same time buoyed up with a sense of anticipation; he wanted to make the decisions and rearrange his life.

Time dragged. He wandered into the area where there were a number of estate agents and again considered various possibilities. He had a half pint in a pub; later he couldn't even remember its name. No more than half a pint as he guessed that there was going to be a lot of booze flowing at the party. After a while he wandered out into the street and on the spur of the moment, he caught a bus heading for the outer parts of the city. His mind dwelt on Anna. Idly watching the scenery, if this drab assemblage of late Victorian housing now giving way to early twentieth century council estates could be described as scenery; he saw a church, one built in the rather debased gothic style of the interwar period. There seemed to be something going on, a small procession was heading out from the church into the side street. Many were elderly, he observed with a wry inward smile, but there were some younger ones. On impulse he got off at the next stop and scurried back to find out what it was about. He caught up with the tail end of the procession. There was a scout band heading it, playing what he realised was a pop song that he couldn't quite recognise, but he knew the words; it was the *Salve Regina*:

> *Hail, holy Queen, Mother of Mercy!*
> *Our life, our sweetness, and our hope!*

It had been adapted somewhat and it was being sung to a catchy tune, at least by some of the people in the procession. Certainly they were younger than most of those attending St. Columba's; was this indeed a way to pull them in? He asked one of the young men, who was wearing a leather jacket, what it was about.

'It's our patronal festival, St Cuthbert's Day. We've had to move it because the Feast was a week last Sunday, but it was more convenient to have it today, especially as it's mid-Lent Sunday tomorrow. Rejoice! Y'know. We are part of the Society of Saint Cuthbert and several of Cuddy's churches join together. We had Mass in our church, now we're walking to Sacred Heart Church.'

'Cuddy?' Steven questioned.

'Pet name of the saint and others with his name.'

Steven was not really surprised that he spoke with a strong local accent; he supposed he must be described as working class. 'Sacred Heart?' he asked. 'Isn't that RC?'

'Yeah! Course we couldn't have done this before, but the RCs are on side now.' He guffawed. 'Me dad used to fight with them after the pubs shut!'

Steven didn't know what to say to that so made a comment about the music. 'Jolly tune, that.' He waved to the head of the procession where the band was.

'Our Vicar wrote that. Well, not the tune, but he adapted the words to it. Great isn't it!'

They soon arrived at Sacred Heart Church, a rather large, barn like structure, typical of the 1930s and all filed in with much clatter and conversation. Once settled the RC priest led the congregation in the Rosary, which seemed to Steven to be interminable. He'd never been an enthusiast for this particular Catholic devotion, but he wished he had some Rosary beads; that would at least give him something to do. A sermon followed; the theme was stepping out in risk and in humility as did Our Lady, so stepping out together as we are today. He somehow linked this to *Strictly Come Dancing.* Then they returned in procession to St. Cuthbert's, for Benediction. The church was a plain, utilitarian building, brick built and of a similar period to Sacred Heart. The tiny sanctuary was flanked by statues of Our Lady and St. Cuthbert and backed by an elaborate painted reredos of the Last Supper. A myriad of candles on the altar and elsewhere twinkled. It was like old times. Once reassembled, there was Benediction with clouds of incense, which created a fog in the tiny church and almost obscured the officiant and his servers. The last hymn *There was a time in England, A time of faith and love*, annoyed and upset him in equal proportions. He had never heard it before, but the thrust was on the blasphemous nature of the reformers' attitude to Eucharistic practice. He ignored it and drifted off into a reverie in which he imagined St. Columba's as it was and he and Anna were kneeling together as they made their marriage vows.

He excused himself from tea and the raffle in the church hall and caught a bus back to the city centre.

★

As arranged, he met her in the foyer of *The Kirkgate*. She greeted him. 'So, what have you been up to, darling?'

He told her what he had done the previous day.

'You went to The Lake District? Poor you!'

'Poor me? But it's beautiful; I kept thinking of you stuck here in Cleadonbridge. It was a lovely day in both senses of the word; I'm sure you would have enjoyed it.'

'Not me, the countryside bores me.'

This was rather depressing, but he was sure that she would change her mind. How could anyone not love the Lakes; he and Mary had enjoyed many happy holidays there and in Snowdonia. But before he had time to remonstrate, he was swept along in the crowd and soon they were in a tiny flat, quite close to Gilbert Street and Lansdowne Terrace. It was the ground floor of one of the smaller terraced houses, which he guessed had been built for lower management. One like this might be a possible place for him to buy, but this was rather run down. He assumed it was on a short term let. The paint was peeling and there was a smell of damp that the mingled odours of after shave and perfume did not fully disguise. They were all packed close together; he could not see Anna.

'Hi, there! I'm Dawn. The drink's in the kitchen.' The speaker gestured towards the rear of the flat. She was a woman of about forty, Steven guessed, clad in what people sometimes termed "ethnic clothes". Her dark hair was very long, hanging to her waist. She had been Mrs. Bankes-Browne in the play. Her manner, rather brash, was not unlike that of the character. 'Do you want to help the kitty?'

'Err, is that for a cat's home or...'

Dawn shrieked with laughter and a rather suave man appeared, somehow from behind her. 'It's a kitty for the booze darling. I'm afraid that neither Dawn nor I can afford to be lavish with the stuff. I'm Ian, by the way.' He extended his hand. Steven saw that he was clad in a close fitting dark blue outfit that rather resembled the shell suits of the '80s. It seemed strangely at variance with Patrick, the character he had played, a golfing companion of Adrian.

Ian saw his stare. 'Do you like this, darling? Oxfam!' He pirouetted dramatically, taking the bowl from Dawn and pushing it towards Steven who chucked a fiver into it. 'You're Anna's friend, aren't you?'

Steven nodded, taking a swig of what he realised was a rather cheap wine. Anna seemed to have disappeared. He supposed that their income would not allow the better wines, although he recalled how he and Mary had long ago decided that a small amount of a good quality wine was better than gallons of plonk.

Graham, who played the part of Adrian, was sitting down. He motioned Steven over. 'Are you a gate crasher, young man?'

Steven did not know quite how to answer this, but Greta moved in. Steven recognised her; she had played the part of the companion to Mrs. Bankes-Browne

'Y'know, young man, it's type casting. She's my minder too. Couldn't manage without her.'

'Course you could!'

Everyone seemed to be talking at once.

'Didn't he get the part of Toby Belch at...'

'No that was old whatisname...'

'When we were at that place near London – you know, commuter town...'

Ian emerged again. 'Are you resting or are you not one of us thesps?'

'Well, I'm actually a retired teacher, but have done a bit of amateur dramatics in the village where I live. I mean we are only amateurs and...'

Ian nodded his approval. 'Some of our finest actors started their careers on the amateur stage. Don't put yourself down. I'm sure you are very good.'

'Come on! Get some music on!' Dawn shouted. A few seconds later the strains of an *ABBA* song were heard. 'Oh not that! It's so yesterday!'

'I first heard it when I was on tour with *Bootlegs* in Cardiff of all places.'

Ian seemed to like it, he sang the chorus line, swaying in time with the beat.

'Oh there you are, darling!' Anna's tone was almost accusatory. He did not know where she had been and why he himself was apparently in the wrong. He had stayed put, where she had left him. 'Come and give me a hand.' She led the way to the front door and down the half dozen steps to the street. 'We've a delivery of pizzas, just arriving.' She opened the door; on the pavement was a delivery man.

'Order for Ashworth?' he asked.

'Right, we'll take them. Here, Steven, you hang on to them while I pay.'

There were about two dozen or so boxes, somewhat incongruously showing the Rialto and a gondola. He knew that Venice is the most well known Italian city, but the pizza belongs to Naples. He smiled as he recalled insisting that he and Mary should not eat pizza when they were in Venice; it is of course widely available there as in every city of the world.

The last words he must have spoken aloud, for Anna, having dismissed the delivery man, said, 'What's in every city of the world, darling?'

'Pizza, but I doubt if it is in Pyongyang… the capital of North Korea, you know.'

'No doubt, but instead of having a medieval dispute can you get them into the back room so that we can eat the blessed things! I've just paid. We collected £7.50 from everyone, so if you've a mind, give me that when you can.'

Here we are! He dumped the boxes on a table beside which was Ben who had played the part of Dave, the drug dealer. As Dave he had a pronounced, almost adenoidal Liverpool accent, so Steven was surprised at Ben's languid drawl. 'Thank you, my good man. You're Anna's fella, aren't you?'

'I think you're rushing things, Ben.' This was from

Marilyn who had been Loopy Lou who was murdered. 'They're just good friends.'

'Oh no,' put in Paula, who played Jacky, the other girl in the drug dealing trio. Steven was amazed now that she did have a Merseyside accent. 'Him and her'll be having a bit of fun, I'm sure.' She almost leered at him.

'Don't be coarse, Paula,' interposed Marilyn.

Steven tried to turn the conversation. 'So, you are actually from Liverpool then?'

'Born and brought up on Scottie Road.'

'Scottie Road?' he questioned.

'Scotland Road, the road to Scotland.'

Ben interposed, 'And the axis of the Irish area of the city.'

'So,' Steven asked, 'were you the language tutor for this play? I loved the way there were subtle differences of accent… Dawn as "posh" but with an accent that slipped, that was wonderful.'

'I tried, but the director insisted on a pro… a professional language coach.'

Ben had suggested he was "Anna's fella", and of course in one sense that was the case as had he not renewed his acquaintance with her, he would have been somewhere else. But she was seldom by his side, instead having animated conversations with the other actors. He heard her now talking to Paula and moved over.

'You don't sound like a local.'

'Oh yes, I was born and brought up here, so getting the flat in Gilbert Street was a sort of homecoming. But Mummy was very strict about speaking "proper"!' She laughed. 'And LAMDA polished my accent!'

'Oh I know both parts of that. Not that I went there or any real drama school, I came in by the back door. But me mam always tried to get us to speak like the radio; she said that was how we should talk but try doing that in a working class environment. Y'd get crucified.'

He tried to but in. 'What's LAMDA?'

'The London Academy of Music and Dramatic Arts.' Anna spoke shortly.

'So how did you two meet?' asked Paula.

Anna raised her hands, the gesture some seemed almost to be fending him off. 'Oh he's part of my past here in Cleadonbridge. He suddenly came crawling out of the woodwork.'

Steven felt rather hurt. Evidently, she did not want to be thought of as his girlfriend, but perhaps there was more to it. Perhaps it was that he had been linked to her through Greg.

It was about 10.30 when they had assembled in the flat and before all the pizzas had been eaten and the wine drunk, it was nearly midnight. As the following day was Sunday, there was no performance, so it seemed as though everyone wanted to let their hair down. It had been an almost exhilarating experience. However, Steven was feeling his age.

Anna detached herself from Paula. 'I'm a bit tired. I love acting, but at my age it does take it out of you, and everyone was noisier than usual, probably because of the play being a bit like that. Do you mind if I go straight back home?'

He agreed. 'Me too.'

As they strolled back in silence towards the area he was

already imagining as home, he spoke tentatively. 'Can we meet tomorrow?' She seemed less tense now; it might be that he could "pop the question" then.

'Mmm, perhaps.'

'I thought of going to St. Peter's for the 11.00 service and then…'

'Why ever do you want to go there? It's not your cuppa tea. Amplified guitars and percussion, loud singing and so on.'

'I want to see.' He knew he was sounding stubborn and expected her to refuse to accompany him, but she surprised him.

'Perhaps I might find it an uplifting experience too, though I doubt it.'

'I want to go to see how that type of service pulls them in and to see if it could be translated to the Anglo Catholic ritual.' This would be a major part of his new life here in Cleadonbridge.

'I'm not sure the idea is translatable.'

They walked on in silence to Gilbert Street. At the entrance to her flat, she turned, kissed him lightly and then inserted the key into the door. 'Bye, Steven, dear!'

Chapter Twelve

Sunday 3rd April 2011

On the Sunday morning, Steven set out for St Peter's along the Boulevard. It was a bright and sunny day and as he walked briskly along, rather later than he had intended, he speculated on what would have been happening, not fifty years ago, when he himself would have been walking in the opposite direction to St. Columba's, but a century earlier, when the area was still one of gracious living. He looked across at the imposing row of houses, built he would guess, in the 1880s, about the time St. Peter's church was built. There was real wealth in the district in those days. Some renovation had occurred, though the number of bells showed subletting. He stopped briefly and counted at one house, twelve, so a dozen households where there had been just one, perhaps the home of a wealthy merchant or a professional man. He glanced at his watch, it was only five minutes to the start of the service and he was still some distance from the church. He quickened his pace. His further musing included those he had known, such as the young Hallworths and Walmsleys who might have been heading to St. Columba's, but there would be others walking in the same direction that he was now. He imagined there would be many bound for church all clad in their best clothes. Remembering the old family photographs he and Mary had of the period, he tried to picture as little girls those he had known as middle aged or elderly ladies. The mothers would have been wearing long dresses and overcoats of shorter length, perhaps with a fox fur. The girls would have shorter dresses and coats with matching cloak around the shoulders. All would have hats; the ones worn by the mothers would be those wide brimmed ones, trimmed, no doubt with some flowers or even feathers. Would they smile politely or ignore the churchgoers moving to the other church? His recollections of his own time here were that they just ignored the others, for there were still a few heading for churches at this time on a Sunday. But that was in a city; it was not like his home village, where everyone seemed to know everyone else, and smiled or greeted passers by. Of course in the village, many in 1911 would be heading to church and now there were far fewer.

Today there were not many people about and none seemed likely to be walking to church, though as he glanced at his watch, he saw that anyone bound for St. Peter's would have reached the church already. He further quickened his pace.

'Steven!' He turned. Much to his surprise it was Anna. 'Are you trying to run away from me?' She was panting. 'As soon as I was catching you up you walked even faster!'

'I'm sorry. I'd no idea you were there. I didn't expect you would come here.'

'I did say I might find it an uplifting experience.'

He grinned. 'I suppose I didn't really believe you were serious.'

'But, darling, I want to help you…' Her voice faded away.

'Help me?'

'Do you mind if we pause a moment, I'm rather out of breath.' She did not explain what she had meant by "help" and the moment passed.

They reached St Peter's only just in time. At the top of the steps they were greeted by a young man who was of student age; his accent suggested that he was not of the locality.

'Hi!' He extended his hand. 'I'm Simon!'

Steven shook Simon's hand and managed a wan smile. 'Steven.'

'And I'm Anna.'

'Your first time at Pete's?' Steven nodded. 'Well, a great welcome!' He ushered them inside.

Steven didn't recall ever visiting the church when he was a student; it was "Low" and thus despised. The building was late Victorian Gothic and with its commanding position at the end of the Boulevard, it had been, and indeed remained, a striking feature of the townscape. In spite of its churchmanship, the design had clearly been influenced by the nascent Anglo Catholic movement and there was a long raised chancel, although this was now obscured by a huge screen onto which the words of the opening hymn were projected. Behind and in semi darkness could be discerned an altar piece of some richness.

'Room here, my friends!' One of the other members of the congregation extended a welcoming hand. Like most of the congregation he was young, though more than student age. Looking round a nearly full church, perhaps a couple of hundred people, there seemed to be more men than women, an odd fact in itself. He looked at the leaflet which gave a structured plan of a non liturgical service. It was difficult to realise that this was the same denomination as St. Columba or his own parish church, St. Mary Magdalene. The Anglican liturgy, either the old Book of Common Prayer or the new flexible Common Worship, seemed to have been abandoned. The children were invited to the front of the church. There must have been a couple of dozen Steven thought. A young man came from the vestry, apparently an ordinary guy, carrying certain tools, one of which he held up.

'What's this?' called the presenter.

'A saw!' chorused the children.

'Who uses a saw?'

'My dad,' volunteered one of the children.

'Is that his job?'

'No, he works in an office.'

'Anyone know what we call someone who works with saws and these?' The presenter nodded to the young man, who then produced a plane and a chisel.

'A joiner?'

'Yes, and there's another word: a carpenter. Jesus was a carpenter and a real friend, mending things…'

'Like my dad mended the rocking horse?' shouted one of the boys.

'Exactly. But,' he said, again nodding to the young man, who now donned a fairly convincing legal wig, 'he's also a… anyone know?'

The was a silence and then someone said, 'He's like one of the men in the law courts.'

'Yes, he's a judge and…' There was another quick change as the man portraying Jesus donned a gold crown.

It looked to Steven as though it might have come from a Christmas cracker, and he giggled silently at the thought. 'So, what is a man who wears this?'

'A king!' shouted several of the children.

'Yes, Jesus is a man like me and your dads, but he is also a Judge and a King. Now Frank is going to take you into the hall where he will tell you all much more about Jesus. Now for all of you, if you look in your Bibles and find Mark's Gospel chapter 14 verse 62.'

Steven noted there was a Bible, the New Internationalist version. He found the text, "And you will see the Son of Man sitting at the right hand of the Mighty One and coming on the clouds of heaven."

Then the children were led off. The idea of judgement seemed worrying, and Steven wondered if, when they were in the church hall, there would be something about hell and its terrors. But all seemed very bright and cheerful. This led into worship song – with loud acoustic guitars, percussion, and a keyboard accompanying hymns with rather banal words. There seemed to be a greater emphasis on Jesus than the other two Persons of the Trinity, but that was, he supposed, typical of Evangelicals. Another reading was now given, from Paul's Epistle to the Romans. The service sheet gave space for one to make notes. Steven's first was, "No consideration of the context of Paul's writing this, or of alternative approaches adopted – this is simply taken as a clear unequivocal and divinely inspired message." It was so different from the questioning attitude of the Vicar of his home parish, who stopped to explain the subtleties of certain phrases in the original Greek, and giving her own views as well as the views of scholars on the meaning of the passage.

This pattern continued for the remainder of the hour. Who was it had described the Free Church services pattern as "a hymn sandwich". Which was the bread and which the meat? Steven giggled.

'Now let us with truly thankful hearts, enjoy God's bounty.' This turned out to be a grace, for without a formal blessing, the service was over, and the congregation filed into the church hall for soup and bread. The soup was vegetable from a packet, but good of its kind and the bread was white sliced loaf. It was easier to feed the… well, not five thousand, but two hundred, with this, rather than with home made soup and wholemeal bread, he supposed.

Simon approached. 'Great to have you with us. Do you live in this area?'

'Not now, but I was a student at the University half a century ago and attended St. Columba's.

'So was St. Columba's a real spiritual home to you?'

'Well it's all a long time ago. Anna still goes there.'

'Not very often, I'm afraid!' she said. 'Excuse me.' She wandered away, chatting to another and rather more intense young man. Steven followed her but felt embarrassed and, glancing at his watch, murmured something about its being time to leave.

'I also do need to be getting on,' said Anna, 'there's something I need to do this afternoon.' With a few brief comments and assurances about returning, they stepped out onto the Boulevard or "escaped", as he later put it.

'It was odd, sort of…' He hesitated.

'A bit too much for you, Steven darling? All the Hallelujah, Jesus loves you?'

'Well, it's not the Church of England as I knew it, or as

I know it today. The old Low Church like our own parish fifty years ago, was not like that, there was a liturgy; it's all so, so…'

'Easy and pat? Just follow this and you're into heaven?'

'I suppose so. It's not as easy as that. And the music is too loud; I'd be deafened if I had much more of it. I suspect that the Alpha Course that they boost is like that and…'

'They make everything too easy; follow all these rules and bingo, Heaven! Like what seems to be the opposite extreme, those who are more Catholic than the Pope.'

'That's what my mother used to say.'

'Your mother must have been a very sensible woman.'

'That's what Mary often said.'

'Oh, I'm sorry. I shouldn't have upset you.'

'No, no, don't worry.' He was silent for a moment.

'But Father Tom is considering using the Alpha Course.'

'Really?'

'It has a wider ranging appeal than you imagine. I am only on the margins of the church, but I did try to tell you the other day that the old divisions are almost meaningless now.'

'I suppose so. The sort of preaching we had there,' he said as he gestured back to St. Peter's, 'isn't new nor is it confined to Evangelical Christianity. It goes back to medieval times if one thinks of the Last Judgements.'

'Like the Sistine Chapel? Every inch of the ceiling and walls swarming with the figures of saints, demons, and everyone in between.'

'You've been there then?'

She nodded. 'I went years ago with Will.' She giggled. 'There's one figure that has just realised that he is damned and is going down. Will suggested that his whole expression was saying, "Oh shit!".'

Steven laughed. 'But I worry about the children. After that introduction to Jesus as Friend, King and Judge, they were led off. What horror stories may they have been told?'

They fell silent and Steven mused that perhaps a trip to Rome as honeymoon might be appropriate. 'Would you want to go to Italy again? he asked, 'go further south, Vedi Napoli e poi muori?!'

'See Naples and die? I'm not sure if the piggy bank would stretch to that, darling.'

Shortly after this they reached the end of Gilbert Street. A perfunctory kiss on the cheek and Anna was off, to get her head down as she put it, and read the script for a new play for which she was to be auditioned.

★

Steven felt rather at a loose end. He wanted to be with Anna but that was impossible for now. He decided that the soup and bread at Pete's was sufficient for lunch, so, deciding that he might as well go for a walk, he turned back towards Belford Park.

Surely this was what was right for him now – not cocooned in a middle class, rural ghetto, but in the beating heart of a city, with Anna. She excited him, made him feel young again and they could work together to pull St. Columba's round. She had said she wanted to help him, but he had not followed it up. If St. Peter's could pull them in with its forms of worship and outreach it could be done elsewhere. Indeed, St. Cuthbert's seemed to be doing so. Last week he had the germ of an idea, now he should develop it. Anna could help; she said she wanted to help.

He had reached the end of the Boulevard and was gazing up at the spire of St. Peter's. There was a poem somewhere about heaven pointing spires; he stood trying to recall it. Perhaps it could be used in the campaign. After all, as Anna had just pointed out, there was no real hostility between the various branches of Anglicanism. We could all work together. There was the Methodist place along the side road, what was it called?

'You all right mate?' The speaker was a man of about fifty who had appeared from nowhere it seemed.

'Yes, I'm fine. I was just thinking about heaven pointing spires, as someone wrote.' Steven laughed apologetically.

'So, Heaven is up there?' The man chuckled, then sang,

There's a Friend for little children
Above the bright blue sky.

'Did all that at Sunday School, there.' He jerked his thumb towards the church. 'Load o' codswallop, ain't it? Eh?'

'Well, of course Heaven cannot be above the bright blue sky, it will be a different sort of... type of... existence, when we will be in the presence of God.'

'Codswallop! Anyway, you're all right, so I'll be on me way.'

As the man walked away, Steven realised that the stranger's action was his concern for another person. He was motivated by Christian charity. Could that be the starting point for a revival? With such muddled thoughts he continued his walk. But that conversation could have been like the road to Damascus for Saul, if only he had used the right words with the stranger.

★

Anna had not suggested that they dine together; later he saw that she had opened a can of baked beans. Steven's walk had given him an appetite, so he asked Catherine if she had a meal available. This time it was Chicken Tikka Masala and he accepted her offer of a bottle of the red wine. It didn't seem to matter about the quality of wine with such spicy food, he thought. Was he trying to summon up Dutch courage?

He then made his way to Anna's flat. She looked preoccupied. He remembered that she had been reading the new play for which she was to audition.

'What's the play like?'

'What play? Oh, the one they are putting on in May?' He nodded. 'It's quite good really, modern lives interwoven with sex and political intrigue. I'm just not sure if I can do it, or rather, if they will cast me in it and I need the money!' She laughed in a slightly embarrassed way.

His mind went racing on. If she was a bit short, then he could help and of course later they would pool their resources and... Aloud he said, 'I can help you out if you need a bit of the ready.'

'I don't need your help, thank you!' She spoke quite forcefully.

'That's all right, it's just that…'

'I'm sorry. I shouldn't have upset you.'

'You said this morning that you came to St. Peter's because you wanted to help me?'

'Did I?'

'Yes. What did you mean?'

'Oh, it was just that you seem on your own and at a loose end, you're looking for something perhaps… I dunno.'

This seemed the moment to turn the subject of the conversation, but Anna's reaction, throwing her arms round him, plunging them into the coupling that he had meant to be the culmination of the evening, when they had agreed to be married, a sort of sealing of the agreement… no he, didn't like that term. Their love making was brief but intense.

'Well Ms Ashworth,' he began, as he retrieved his shoes, kicked carelessly into the further corners of the living room, for they had not made it to the bedroom.

'Well? It was very well, my darling.' Anna was fastening the straps of her bra as she spoke, and Steven was tying his shoe laces so no contact was possible. She lay back, still without her blouse. 'I'm exhausted. This is the moment when in the old films they lit their post coital cigarettes.'

'Did you ever smoke? I can't remember.'

'I didn't when you knew me. When I was living at home, though Mummy was a veritable chimney if you recall; she couldn't have objected. Actually, I vowed as I listened to her coughing every morning that I wouldn't, but in the theatre almost everyone did then. Daddy never did. Oddly enough it was something that Will said which made me give up.' She smiled at the recollection. 'He bet

163

me I couldn't give up and I shouted at him that he'd never be able to give up. In the end we both did, neither of us wanting to allow the other to win.'

'Mary and I decided to give up years ago, before it became fashionable to do so. It's ironic that she died of cancer.' They were sitting side by side on the settee and Anna laid her hand on his. 'It must have been difficult for your parents, one smoking and the other not, I mean.' He turned to her and pressed his lips to hers. 'It's not nice kissing a smoker if you aren't one yourself.'

She returned his kiss very gently. 'That's true.'

'So if we were to, err… be together, that wouldn't be a difficulty between us.' He raised his eyebrows and pressed her hand more tightly.

She looked baffled. 'What do you mean, "together"?'

'If we were to, well, if we were to get married.'

'So that's what you are planning, Mr. Darlington!' Her expression was indefinable.

'A nice Catholic ceremony at St. Columba's and a honeymoon in the Lake District, perhaps in Keswick, or even', he hesitated, 'Italy. I'd have pots of money so we could buy a really nice property and you could…'

'I could what?'

'Well I don't know, you might want to keep this place on, and we could live in the country somewhere, though if we were in Cleadonbridge we could help St. Columba's.'

'Help? In what way?'

'Well, help to supplement, rather than replace the evangelical thrust of places like St. Peter's. You agree that St Peter's is too simplistic; you love the old ritual tempered by modernism and with a little bit of money we could help put St. Columba's back on its feet. I wouldn't want to be Forward in Faith like St. Cuthbert's but they are pulling in the younger ones with the full Catholic ritual. You know, yesterday afternoon we sang *Salve Regina*, adapted somewhat to a pop tune. And there was this chubby working class lad in a leather jacket; well he was about thirty I suppose, delighting in it. Apparently the Vicar, or did he say their parish priest… anyway it was a locally grown product, the *Salve Regina* that is.' He smiled.

'Leaving aside the fact that I don't believe all this is possible, and that perhaps you should not be throwing your money after a lost cause, which your boys would have something to say about. I'd guess…' She paused. 'How many of the people in the procession at St. Cuthbert's were young and working class?'

'Not many I suppose…'

'So you are erecting a whole hypothesis of Catholic renewal in the inner city on the basis of one lad in a leather jacket? I don't want to be cruel; I know you are well meaning, but I think you'll find that the St. Peter's lot are very earnest young people from middle class backgrounds, who are come to convert the inner city. It's naïve to imagine that it can be done, and you are naïve to imagine St Columba's can be a sort of Catholic bastion against it, because that's what you think you want, isn't it? But in any case, you are forgetting something.'

'What's that?' he asked.

'You seem to imagine that the majority are still believers. I doubt if that was ever the case, but now, most are indifferent, plus the fact that what is done, either in the most incense swinging, holy water scattering High Mass or in the loud cymbal banging temples of Evangelical fervour, is completely meaningless to them.'

'Meaningless?'

'In a few weeks it will be Easter. For most people it means a nice spring break with Easter Eggs and so on. If they think at all about the Resurrection, which most won't, they are not likely to think it is credible. Which bishop talked about "a conjuring trick with bones"?'

'David Jenkins, Bishop of Durham in the 1980s sometime.' Steven was prompt in his reply. 'But he went on to say that the resurrection was real but was not that simple and...'

Anna interrupted him. 'None of the people out there,' she said as she swept her hand around in a dramatic gesture, 'will understand the niceties of theological language. It is either a reanimation of a dead body, which they cannot accept, or it's a massive piece of codology.'

'But...' He remembered the conversation he had had outside St. Peter's that afternoon with the man who had used that same word; he realised that probably Anna was right.

There was a pause. 'But in a way it is worse than that,' said Anna. 'Most simply don't care. You know the doctrine of the Eucharist. You know the doctrine of the Atonement and so on. Do you think many people believe the idea that... well, think of the hymn you'll almost certainly sing on Good Friday.' She recited:

> There was no other good enough
> To pay the price of sin;
> He only could unlock the gate
> Of heaven and let us in.

'The price of sin? A wrathful God who demands a blood sacrifice?'

'It isn't quite like that, it's…' He hesitated.

'Do you believe it all?' He made no reply. 'Do you?' She persisted.

'I see it as a sort of myth, that…'

'The time has passed for theological discussion. All I was trying to point out that it is an impossible task to re-evangelise Cleadonbridge or anywhere else for that matter.'

'What do you think then?'

'In any case, I doubt that you realise just how much it would cost to put St. Columba's "back on its feet" as you say.'

'But if we were able to develop some outreach work and I could get involved…'

'Even if it were possible, you aren't the right person to lead something like this; you come from outside, both in regional and class terms. It's different for clergy; they are expected to be middle class and so on. And you seem to have taken it for granted that I will share in this.'

'Well if we were to get married…'

'You mentioned that before.'

'Well we have… had…' He was at a loss for the right word. The conventional "made love" seemed almost a euphemism; the other terms were either coarse or clinical.

'We've shagged, you mean?'

He winced. 'If you want to put it like that, yes I suppose so.'

She drew a deep breath. 'I'm guessing here. Did you and Mary ever go to bed before you were married?' He shook his head. 'I thought so. And have you ever strayed from the straight and narrow?'

Again, he shook his head. 'I've never had sex with anyone else until the other night and it seemed…'

'I think you may be living in another world, my dear.' He looked baffled. 'A world of monogamy, of lifetime fidelity, not that such ever really existed, except in the pious hopes of a few. Do you think… I am putting words into your mouth here, that because we have had sex together, we are sort of committed?'

'I suppose I do, but not because we have to.' He tried to lighten the conversation. 'Like the old "have to get married" when the girl was pregnant. I'd thought we got on; we had so much in common and…' His voice trailed away. 'I suppose not, but…'

'What things do you think we have in common? The other day you admitted that you would rather go wandering over the hills that tread the boards.' She looked hard at him.

'Well yes, but I do love the theatre, at least when it is a good play. The one that you are hoping to be cast in sounds really worthwhile.'

'Maybe. But whereas we might have that in common there is no way I could ever countenance living anywhere other than a city, and no way will I do more than admire the mountains from the inside of a warm car, or from the window of an hotel. Even that would bore me after a couple of days.'

'But we've just…'

'An occasional meeting, perhaps with sex if we both want it, that is OK. You and Mary had a great marriage; I could envy you and I am certainly sorry for you that it was cut short. But I am not Mary.' She relaxed a little. 'Though you imagined me to be her that first time.'

'That was awful. How can you forgive me?'

She brushed it away in a gesture. 'Don't let it upset you. But it is perhaps, very significant.' She paused. 'Do you know what I think you are trying to do, subconsciously perhaps?'

'No, tell me.'

She spoke harshly. 'You are manipulating me, trying to make me like your poor, dear, dead wife. I'm not like her and Cleadonbridge is not like your village in Devon. Nor could you work the miracle of reviving St. Columba's.'

There was a silence before more gently she spoke again. 'Steven dear,' she laid her hand on his arm as if in restraint. 'You don't really belong here. It's just not practicable.'

He walked back to *The Osborne* feeling flattened. Involvement with this area had seemed a real possibility, involvement with Anna even more exciting... it could have been the beginning of a new life; a life that would be far away from the stuffy old place where he had been born and which he had chosen to spend almost all his life. He might have had excitement in the city, but perhaps Anna was right, there was no place for him here; there's no fool like an old fool. That poem came back, this was indeed no country for old men, at least this old man.

Next week he would go home to Devon.

Chapter Thirteen

Monday 4th April 2011

Steven decided to leave Cleadonbridge the following day, making his apologies to Catherine Jones and collecting his things together as quickly as possible. As he expected, there was no problem about getting a seat on the train, although he had not booked. He felt disappointed, almost humiliated and he neither watched the passing scenery nor read as the train took him closer to Devon. His confused thoughts were interrupted by the announcement.

'The next station will be…' He was home, or he soon would be. "The rich man in his castle…" He recalled his thoughts the night he had met Luke and Josh in *The Pen and Wig* the previous week. This place was not as liberal as the city and yet there was a settled order, an order, of which he was a part. He hauled his rucksack off the rack and made his way to the door of the train.

The railway station is in the valley a few minutes' walk away from the town centre which is on a hill. He smiled inwardly; some described the place as a town; its market charter had been granted in the thirteenth century, the first citizen was a mayor and High Street was lined with shops, which at one time sold some of the finest goods; some of them still made a brave effort. He did patronise them sometimes, but today he hardly noticed the features of the street. In the opinion of many, the population of a little over five thousand meant it was no more than a village.

He paused before setting off up the lane that led off High Street to where the urban features of the medieval core, strung out along the original main road gave way to a more suburban townscape where houses such as *Green Haugh* had been built. His thoughts over the past few days had been that Cleadonbridge was right for him… in the heart of a city, with Anna. But was his home town indeed a middle class rural ghetto.

'You are still miles away!'

He was startled, and then smiled. It was Susan Jamieson. He was home. He had to stand for a little while and hear her chatter, first about how she had checked on the house and garden, then the usual stuff about village matters.

'…and we do hope that you'll be doing something in it in summer!'

'What sort of thing, Susan?'

'Well, some sort of pageant or tableau if not a play. We could leave it to you people in the drama group.' The Vicar was talking about it and as she knew I was in touch with you she asked me to ask you when you came back… to get you involved.' She paused and looked at Steven expectantly.

It might have been the church or the village festival. He should have listened more. Perhaps if he simply nodded and let her ramble on… 'When is it again?'

'The patronal festival of course, or at least as near it as we can make it. This year is probably the 750th anniversary of the church.'

That was it then, church and the dedication was to St. Mary Magdalene and the Feast day was July 22nd so there was just about time. What was Susan saying?

'So, if we could have some sort of play about her. Do you know of one?'

'I don't know any. It might be interesting to try to find one.' But his mind was racing on. Could he write a play? There was only a short time, three and a half months to organise it. He had written something, a one act play for the anniversary of the market charter, creating supposedly medieval characters who were in reality twentieth century small town citizens. He managed a fairly convincing cod "Olde Worlde" language too. What did we know about Mary Magdalene? She was one of Jesus' followers and was present at two of the most important moments: his crucifixion and resurrection. What was it that Jesuit had said in those talks in Exeter that he had attended, a sort of side reference to Rome's reluctance to allow women to be ordained? She had the title "Apostle to the Apostles" that St. Augustine gave her. He had recalled the wonderful economy of the Latin *Apostola Apostolorum*, with its clear indication that she was female apostle to the male apostles, for she gave them the glad news of the Resurrection. Then there was that bit about "seven demons" sometimes interpreted as referring to complex illnesses. Then of course Mary as the reformed prostitute, or even Jesus' lover as in *The Da Vinci Code*, but he had read somewhere that there was no evidence to suggest the former, still less the latter. How about involving the Vicar, Wendy? Or of course, Mary Magdalene must be in the medieval mystery plays; they would give a ready made script and would involve several dozen people, that in itself would be an opportunity and yet a problem, though the fact that many of the actors would be rather wooden might even be typical of the original. His mind raced on. 'I must go and sort my things out.'

'Are you sure you don't need anything now? I could do your washing or something. When you rang me this morning to say you were on your way, I ran a duster round and hoovered the carpets; it would be no trouble as I can do your things with mine!'

'It's awfully kind of you, but really there's no need.' He was always embarrassed by her helpfulness; but there was an additional reason for her not seeing his clothing. He wasn't absolutely sure that there would be no tell tale signs of his coupling with Anna the other night; not that she would gossip, at least he didn't think she would, but he would rather she didn't see anything.

He averted his eyes from the garden where weeds were, no doubt, starting to grow, dumped his bag in the hall and made a cup of tea. Suitably refreshed, he sallied forth to the SPAR shop to find something for dinner. The street, although not unduly busy, seemed to have people he knew from all aspects of life over… heavens, it might almost be described as three quarters of a century.

There was David Rollins; they had been at primary school together, but he had missed the eleven plus. This meant that he remained in the all age school, which served the village before the secondary modern, now a comprehensive school, had been built in the late 1950s. The school had not, he felt sure, offered a much of an education, but David had prospered and was now running a successful building firm. They waved cheerily to each other across the village street.

Mrs. Watson appeared from the short lane that led to the old peoples' bungalows. She had known his mother and Steven imagined that she was of a similar age, although his mother would now be in her late '90s. 'Good afternoon, Mrs. Watson. How nice to see you!'

'Steven! I won't say I mustn't grumble; it's so tiresome. I'm really remarkably well considering I shall be 95 next month. I can get about as you see! I'm on my way to the shop.'

'Me too. I'll walk along with you.'

'And how are you?'

They chatted as they walked slowly down the street.

'Y'know, as you get older the years seem to fly by. Mind you, I can remember your mother pushing you out in the pram, so proud of you she was. I'd had three of my four by then and I sometimes think she and your poor dear father had given up hope of having any babies.'

'You'll remember Auntie Maggie, of course?'

'Of course. She rather frightened me.'

Steven chuckled. 'She frightened me. If ever I had to go into the shop, she looked at me as though I were something the cat brought in. I think it was to do with the fact that Dad and the others didn't want to take over the business that George and his brothers had built up. Her hanging onto the shop here was a sort of act of defiance.'

'Well Jim Andrews is a lot easier to chat to. As was his father when he took over after Maggie died. Well, here we are at the shop. I'll see you in church on Sunday of course.'

'Yes, there's something I want to chat to Wendy about, though it might be better if I saw her sooner.'

'I suppose she's right, the Vicar, I mean. She says Christians ought to use Christian names, but I find it difficult. I mean it was bad enough when they appointed a lady as Vicar, though she is very good, and I can accept her now, but I cannot bring myself to call her "Wendy", and I know she wants to call me Catherine, but… oh I don't know. Mind you, I think your Auntie Maggie would have refused to darken the door of the church if there'd been a lady vicar appointed. I wonder what you own mother would have thought.'

'I sometimes wonder that myself, but it was only being discussed when she died. She didn't like the idea. Anyway, I'll just do a quick whisk round, get myself something to eat. I've been away for a few days.'

'I know, Susan Jamieson told me all about it. You're all right then, living on your own up there?'

His immediate reaction was to be angry at the implication that he should move, as of course she had after her husband's death over twenty years ago, but he realised she was motivated solely by concern for him. He forced a smile. 'I really am fine, thanks, Mrs. Watson.' He selected a ready meal, decided to treat himself to a bottle of half decent red wine and some of the local cheese. He bought some yoghurt and would use some of the fruit in the freezer with it. A feast!

At the till Betty, who made teas at drama group productions tackled him. 'Michael tells me you am't in the play next month. Why's that? You are the best one they've got!'

'I wanted a break…'

'Of course, with your Mary dying last year and all. I'm

175

sorry, m'dear.' She patted his hand. That of course wasn't the reason, or perhaps it was, he thought.

As he walked out of the shop he almost bumped into Penny Brookes, secretary of the garden society.

'I'm glad I met you, Steven. It's a pity you weren't here at the meeting last week.'

He felt guilty and was about to apologise, but she continued.

'We discussed having an open garden event at the time of the plant sale in May, instead of paying for the village hall fees; they've put them up again, you know, we could have it in a member's garden and have other gardens open too. *Green Haugh* is the obvious place. Would you consider opening it for the sale?'

'Let me think about it, Penny! What's the date?'

'Probably the second Saturday in May; we'd want to avoid the Bank Holidays.'

What was the line in that poem? *No country for old men…* Wasn't this the place, the country for him, not Cleadonbridge? He was of some use here; he couldn't be in the city. The garden would need attention, especially if he were to open it for the plant sale, as Penny had suggested. Then there was the play he might write or adapt, and church matters were looming large. Wendy had suggested a massive outreach programme to which Michael, the Treasurer had pointed out that there was little money in the church account and some massive fund raising would be needed. Wendy had said, quite forcefully, that if the outreach increased active membership there would be more on the plate, each Sunday. Help would be needed there.

Chapter Fourteen

Thursday 5th July 2012

The Belleville was on the edge of the city's commercial district, tucked away in a side street next to the main line railway station. Steven had never really noticed it when he was a student and now, as he waited in the entrance hall for the others to join him, he speculated on its origin. It might have been a fairly substantial house, or perhaps it had been built as a more modest hotel, for those who could not afford *The Royal Station*, the palatial establishment built by the railway company. It was a pleasant, mild evening and as it was daylight, he wandered outside to take a closer view.

'Hey!' Steven turned. It was, as he might have guessed, Dorothy. 'We were told,' she again spoke as though to a wayward child, 'to meet in the foyer at half past. It's only twenty past and you are out here on the street.'

'I was just looking at what the hotel looked like from the outside and wondering whether it was built as an hotel.'

Dorothy's tone now became more that of a teacher who is pleased with her star pupil. 'Now I do know that. I found an old Bradshaw and it seems it was the *Commercial Hotel*, rather cheaper than *The Royal Station*. I suppose *Belleville* sounds better.'

They moved back into the hotel to wait for the others, who had begun to arrive. 'Black tie,' Frank had stated and the men were all wearing dinner jackets. It always seemed illogical that whereas men were almost in uniform, women had the freedom to choose colour, length, and style. Dorothy was clad in a slim line royal blue dress and was carrying a very dark blue handbag, which matched her shoes. Barbara Applethwaite, however, was in tweed.

There was a buzz of conversation. Promptly, at 7.30, Frank appeared. 'Right, me hearties. If we set off now,' he said and glanced at his watch, 'we should make it to the *Amalthia* in time for an aperitif before our banquet.'

Steven leaned towards Anthony Davies. 'Is he going to suggest we synchronise our watches?'

Anthony chuckled. 'But what on earth is an *Amalthia*?' he asked.

'Now I looked that one up,' Steven replied. 'There is a resort in Crete of that name, and I suspect that's what they had in mind when they named their restaurant, but it actually means to soften or to soothe. In Greek mythology, Amalthia was a goat who nursed the infant Zeus.'

'You were always a fund of useless knowledge.' Anthony laughed.

'The Internet is wonderful thing!'

'What's their marketing ploy there then?' This was from Bob Roberts who was beside them as they walked out into the street.

That would be his take on it, thought Steven. He smiled at Bob. 'Your guess is better than mine on that.'

When they had been students, Tileyard Street and the area around it had been rather broken down, with old industrial buildings, houses that had once been rather grand, but which were boarded up or were slums. A few shops, pubs and perhaps a chip shop or two, were the only active businesses. Steven had not been there the previous year and was amazed at the transformation. Trendy restaurants, small independent shops selling a wide variety of craft and other goods were interspersed with a dozen or more restaurants. The *Amalthia* was on two levels, one was up a short flight of stairs from street level, below this Steven could see another area in a semi basement.

'This way, folks!' Frank led the way up the stairs to the bar. 'Now first drinks are on our genial millionaire, so order an aperitif, and perhaps a bottle or three for the meal.'

Steven ordered a sherry. He was pleasantly surprised that they had a really dry one available. The area just beyond the bar was rather dark and it took Steven a moment to adjust his eyes. Then he noticed a familiar person at a table just round the corner from the bar. They recognised each other immediately.

'Steven darling!' It was Anna.

He was embarrassed. 'Anna. How nice to see you again.'

'Maureen, this is Steven. You remember, I told you about him. Steven, this is Maureen, one of *The Kirkgate* company.'

'Pleased to meet you, Maureen.' She was a similar age to Anna, but rather dowdy by comparison with her companion. Her dress was rather long and in a drab colour, her hair was a sort of mousy brown but was greying at the roots. Anna was in a simple but striking dress of black with stripes of white. Her long hair was flowing. Maureen extended her hand and smiled winningly, which

179

transformed her whole appearance. Steven shook her hand.

'What are you doing here? Have you come back to Cleadonbridge to see me?' Anna's manner was almost seductive, and he became aware of Bob's presence, close behind him.

He introduced them to Bob. 'This is Anna; we used to know each other, and Maureen. They are both actors with *The Kirkgate*.'

'No, dear,' put in Maureen, 'I am in wardrobe; I could never act.'

'And the theatre couldn't do without you and your little band,' said Anna.

'This is Bob. He and I were at university together all those years ago.'

There was a mutual shaking of hands.

'Come along, folks,' shouted Frank. 'When you've got your drinks it's this way, we have the executive dining room booked for our party!' Most of the others had already gone up to the dining room.

'We're here for a reunion, fifty years on from our graduation,' Steven explained, feeling somewhat embarrassed.

'Will you find time to come round and see me?'

'I'm not sure. We are having a meal here and then...'
He turned to Bob, who was hovering, listening.

'Has Frank anything planned for later?'

'I don't think so.'

'Well, you know where I live, if you want to drop in for coffee?' There was a suggestive tone. 'I am "resting" as they say, so I am quite fancy free.' She beckoned him closer and lowered her voice. 'I actually work here to get a few extra pennies, and I was given a staff voucher for me and a friend for a weeknight. I couldn't have afforded it otherwise. But if it's, let's say, the right side of 11.00 you'd be welcome.'

'You're well in there Stevie!' He and Bob had now moved away to join the others.

'What do you mean?' He affected an innocent air.

'She obviously fancies you. I guess you've met her before?'

He was tempted to tell Bob to mind his own business, but he decided to play along with it, a little. 'I have met her before, Bob.'

'She might be the answer to your prayers!'

They had now reached the long tables set out for the party. Steven was glad that there were no two places together which meant he couldn't continue this conversation with Bob.

He found himself between Anthony Davies and Barbara Applethwaite. 'Who was the woman you were chatting to?' asked Barbara. 'She seems very lively.'

'I knew her all those years ago when we were here; she and her parents went to the same church, St. Columba's you know.'

'Did you and her have an affair?' This was from Anthony.

'No, she was Greg Thomas's girlfriend. Did you know him? Read Economics?'

'The name rings a bell, but I can't remember a face.'

'Oh, I can,' put in Barbara, 'I did Economics subsid., you remember. He was a bit of a bully, well, verbally. He had a local girlfriend I recall. So that was her?' She gestured towards the entrance.

Their chat was interrupted by the arrival of a waiter. 'Are you ready to order, madams, sirs?'

'I'm not sure,' said Barbara. 'Starters…let me see. Mmmm, yes *Dolmades* sas parakaloúme.'

The waiter grinned at her use of Greek. 'And you, sir?' He turned to Anthony.

'Not sure… what's *Dolmades*? Oh, I see, stuffed vine leaves, no…'

'I'm going to have *Spanakopita*,' Steven announced. He turned to the waiter. 'That's what, spinach and feta cheese pastries, isn't it?'

'It's all Greek to me!' Anthony spoke almost despairingly then grinned. 'But let's have some wine.'

'The wine list is on the back, sir!'

'Oh, let's go for the house plonk. They come from a small winery in the Peloponnese region,' Anthony read. 'One red and one white here, please.'

'Oh, the Peloponnesus.' Barbara smiled wistfully. 'Roy and I went there on our honeymoon.'

'Ah!' Steven said. 'Of course, Roy Simpson. He was a classicist, wasn't he? I remember you and he were going out together. So you got married. How is he?'

'He died ten years ago.' She spoke in a matter of fact way.

'I'm sorry. I lost Mary two years ago.'

An uncomfortable silence fell over their part of the table.

'We had a lot of good times, many in Greece. Efcharistó!' This was to thank the waiter who had brought the wine. 'We visited all sorts of sites of antiquity, but his other passion was railways, and the Peloponnesus had a lot of lovely steam hauled narrow gauge lines then.'

'So that's why you speak Greek.'

'Only a bit. I left it all to Roy, although there are major differences between modern Greek and the classical language. I suppose it's like the difference between Latin and Italian.'

'Mary and I were always going to go to Greece, but we never got around to it somehow. We often went to France.'

Eddie Saunders, who was sitting opposite, now joined the conversation. 'Helen and I have a camper van and travel a lot on the continent. Mind you, last summer we went to South America. The Iguaçu Falls are amazing. We'd been to Canada in 2000 and saw Niagara but it's nothing compared to Iguaçu.'

'How about the Victoria Falls?' asked Dorothy, leaning across from a few places further along the table.

'I've not been there.'

Steven smiled inwardly; this was place name dropping, in the way that some mentioned titled people of their acquaintance. Their conversation was stilled by the arrival of the starters. Curiously, main course orders had not been placed at the same time and there was some delay after they had finished the starters before they ordered. Steven chose *Afelia*, which was casseroled pork in red wine. Anthony decided on *Stefado Vothino*, a rich beef stew.

'All good macho meals,' Barbara commented as she chose vegetable *Moussaka*. 'I cannot imagine veggie *Moussaka* in Greece; I thought I'd try it.'

Steven felt more integrated into the party than he had earlier in the day. It was a relief that people were not raking over their shared past as students, but talking about recent journeys, Further down the table he could hear an animated discussion on politics was taking place; he was glad he was far away from it. This was perhaps a country for old men, but once tomorrow came they would all be dispersed to other places, far away from Cleadonbridge.

More wine was ordered, conversation flowed. Steven recalled something almost poetic. It was that guy who did that presentation at a wine tasting in the village hall. He came from a wine merchant in Exeter. "Drinking good wine with good food in good company is one of life's most civilised pleasures." He and Mary had enjoyed that idea, and often quoted it at each other. But now he and Mary could not... he then remembered that Anna was in the next room, and he had wanted to share it with her. No, that was foolishness.

Tourta Chokolatas, Baklava... all the desserts, or, as they now were usually named, puddings, seem very sweet, Steven thought. He chose *Pagoto Vanilla*, which was vanilla ice cream.

'It won't be as good as the pistachio ice cream Roy and I had on Aegina,' said Barbara, 'that's an island in the Saronic Gulf.' She added, 'Some sorts of foods bring back memories, don't they?'

He thought for a moment. 'I remember how Mary and I came off Carrauntoohil, the highest mountain in Ireland, you know, on a pouring wet day, longing for tea, not just the cup that cheers but a full afternoon tea.'

'Like those that one got at the *Old Dungeon Ghyll*, where we went with the Rambling Club?' Dorothy put in.

'Three shillings and six pence they cost.'

'You have an incredible memory.'

'But all the good Mrs. Murphy had that wet day was homemade rhubarb tart and cream.'

'Not the same.'

'No. But rhubarb tart always makes me think of that day; we'd done the full Coomloughra Horseshoe, a pretty tough trek.' He laughed. 'I couldn't do it now.'

'Like me,' said Barbara, 'pistachio ice cream and Roy.'

All these were memories of his happy life with Mary. They had never had afternoon tea together at the *Old Dungeon Ghyll*, but they had had all sorts of similar experiences in the Lakes and elsewhere. Absurdly, he had imagined he might enjoy the same sort of life with…

As if on cue, Anna stuck her head round the door of their private room. 'We're off now,' she said, 'I hope I'll see you later then.'

'I could ring you on my mobile if I have a chance.'

After the puddings came coffee.

'I don't want Greek coffee,' said Anthony, 'it's just too sweet.'

'You can ask for it not to be sweetened, *sketo*,' said Barbara.

'Better to have Americano. Do you do that?' asked Steven as the waiter came up.

'Certainly sir! So, all of you for americanos?'

'*Sketo* for me,' said Barbara, 'and let's have some *Ouzo*! The night is young!'

Steven had first heard about *Ouzo* when the drama group at home had decided to put on *Barefoot in the Park*, by Neil Simon. He couldn't remember the play well, but the characters had got drunk on this and he had to look it up to find what it was.

'What is *Ouzo*?' Anthony asked. 'I thought I'd have a brandy.'

Barbara explained. 'It's a dry aniseed drink made in Greece from distilled spirit. It tastes not unlike sambuca that you may have had in Italy, or,' she said and laughed, 'in an Italian restaurant.'

'Let's try it then,' shouted Eddie. 'Waiter!' He waved his hand.

Steven had not liked it when he had tried it before but everyone seemed to be joining Eddie, so he allowed the waiter to pour him a generous measure.

They had all drunk too much and, although they had paid for the "Banqueting Menu" in advance and Bob had stood the cost of the aperitifs, the rest of the wines had to be paid for and it took some time to apportion the cost and find the cash to pay. It was well after 11.00 when they were leaving the restaurant. He couldn't phone Anna now.

It was not until the next day when he was on the train bound for home that he tried and was relieved it was her answer phone. 'Hello, Anna? It's Steven. I'm sorry I just couldn't get to you until about the witching hour, well, that's midnight, isn't it?' Had I gone to see Anna, he thought, it would have been about getting a quick shag, no more. He recalled his return from the earlier trip to Cleadonbridge and the realisation that where he belonged is the little town that had been his home for almost all his life.

Chapter Fifteen

Friday 6th July 2012

He arrived home in the late afternoon. As he walked up the hill from the station and onto the High Street, he thought how in the intervening fifteen months since his last return from Cleadonbridge he had immersed himself in the affairs of his native town and put from his mind everything that had happened in the north.

The Mystery Play had occupied much of his time after he had returned from Cleadonbridge. It had seemed that none of the actual medieval ones was appropriate, so he had written one in a modern form but following the basic ideas of the medieval ones with tableaux created on a trailer, which was pulled by Cyril Aldred's tractor. Cyril was a Roman Catholic so there was a suitably ecumenical dimension. Wendy, the Vicar, had been delighted to take on the part of Mary Magdalene. Many other parishioners and other people of the community had joined in, including some who had no real connection with the Church. His thoughts on the Saint's rôle in the Gospel he had translated in to six scenes, all quite short and taking place at various places along the High Street. Initially she was seen as one of a crowd, following Jesus, played in a rather enigmatic manner by Norman, her husband.

Steven paused now, outside the pharmacy where the tableau of Mary's cure was set.

'Hello, Steven. How are you?' It was Jim Andrews, the pharmacist.

'I'm fine thanks. Just recalling last year.'

'Last year?'

'The mystery play…'

'Oh yes, Wendy feigning a sort of hysterical attack, then Norman stopping and going into the pharmacy, then me coming out, carrying a suitable potion, for Norman to give to Wendy.'

'It was supposed to be for the seven devils that Jesus cast out,' Steven explained.

'Ah yes, you told me at the time. I asked you what they were, and you didn't know, but guessed some sort of mental issue.'

'But you didn't have to add that unscripted line. It was supposed to be a serious play.'

'What? Oh, my saying it was better than Valium. Well, it is, it's a good herbal remedy.'

Further along he reached *Natural Skin Care* run by Angela Thompson. She had been horrified at the thought of one of her special preparations being poured over Norman's feet as Mary Magdalene had over the feet of Jesus. They compromised; the contents of a jar of an inferior product had been transferred to an empty jar of her "exclusive skin care".

He had not been sure if the rather pompous Frederick Roberts, a churchwarden, who was a retired bank manager and a former magistrate, could cope with being Pontius Pilate. He adopted much the same manner as Steven guessed he would have done in court.

'You claim to be King of the Jews? This seems to have no factual basis, young man.'

At the bottom of the path leading to the church, where the final scenes were enacted, he recalled how the crucifixion and internment had been difficult to stage. The resurrection was beside the church; they had left the trailer behind and had carried Norman into the crypt which had an entrance from the churchyard, on the northern side of the building. Beyond here the graveyard sloped steeply upwards and the acoustics seemed to work well.

Some of the year seven pupils from the school had been drafted in as angels to sing to a tune adapted by Kay, the church organist.

Mary, go, tell Peter and the rest of his disciples as He said,
He will go to Galilee, and will meet them there.
You are now the first of the apostles.

Norman had then changed into his work gear; he ran a garden design business and Mary Magdalene had initially assumed that the risen Jesus was a gardener. There had been some giggles when Wendy, as Mary Magdalene said to her husband, 'Good sir gardener, if you have seen Jesus my Lord, where is he now? Can you tell me where he is? I'll give you all I own.'

The reply, 'Mary, tell them I will come to Galilee, and you must bring the Good News from me to all, especially Peter,' led into her slipping off the first century Palestinian robe to reveal her garb as a priest of the Church of England and proclaiming how that Good News, the Gospel, had been proclaimed here for seven hundred and fifty years.

He slipped through the churchyard now to reach *Green Haugh.* This was his native land; some, at least, of his ancestors were here at the time the church was consecrated. There had been gardening to do and with some help from Norman he had tackled a difficult feature in the lower part of the garden. There was no longer any reason to avert his eyes and the soft fruit was producing a wonderful crop. What had prompted him to sort out the problems last year had been his agreeing to take Penny Brookes' suggestion to join in the Open Garden Scheme. People had flooded into his garden and bought the scones which various ladies had made, spread with the jam made from his own fruit, and it had helped to raise the sum of nearly £1000.

This year the early summer had been so full of similar activities that he had little time to consider what he might have missed and by the time of the reunion he had almost forgotten his foolishness of the previous year. But the chance meeting with Anna had caused turmoil in his mind.

Had Anna tried to get in touch? He had used his mobile at the start of the train journey and had not switched it on since. There might be a message on the landline, or an e-mail, he thought. Dumping his bag in the hall, he switched his mobile on, picked up the landline and switched on the computer. He waited. There was nothing. 'Well,' he said aloud to the empty house. 'That's a relief! It's all over. No more silly ideas. It was an old man's fancy.' He recalled the poem by Yeats and its first line which seemed so appropriate. *That is no country for old men*. And yet, and yet… as he mused, the phone rang.

'Hello, Steven dear.'

'Hello Anna.'